More Favorites by
CHRIS GRABENSTEIN

Escape from Mr. Lemoncello's Library
Mr. Lemoncello's Library Olympics
Mr. Lemoncello's Great Library Race
The Island of Dr. Libris
Welcome to Wonderland: Home Sweet Motel
Welcome to Wonderland: Beach Party Surf Monkey

THE HAUNTED MYSTERY SERIES
The Crossroads
The Demons' Door
The Zombie Awakening
The Black Heart Crypt

COAUTHORED WITH JAMES PATTERSON
Daniel X: Armageddon
Daniel X: Lights Out
House of Robots
House of Robots: Robots Go Wild!
House of Robots: Robot Revolution
I Funny
I Even Funnier
I Totally Funniest
I Funny TV
I Funny: School of Laughs
Jacky Ha-Ha
Pottymouth and Stoopid
Treasure Hunters
Treasure Hunters: Danger Down the Nile
Treasure Hunters: Secret of the Forbidden City
Treasure Hunters: Peril at the Top of the World
Treasure Hunters: Quest for the City of Gold
Word of Mouse

SANDAPALOOZA SHAKE-UP

• Book 3 •

CHRIS GRABENSTEIN

illustrated by **Kelly Kennedy**

Random House 🏠 New York

For Fred,
my best four-legged writing partner

Text copyright © 2018 by Chris Grabenstein
Cover art copyright © 2018 by Brooklyn Allen
Interior illustrations copyright © 2018 by Kelly Kennedy

Visit us on the Web! rhcbooks.com

Educators and librarians, for a variety of teaching tools,
visit us at RHTeachersLibrarians.com

Library of Congress Cataloging-in-Publication Data
Names: Grabenstein, Chris, author. |
Kennedy, Kelly (Illustrator), illustrator.
Title: Sandapalooza shake-up / Chris Grabenstein ;
illustrated by Kelly Kennedy.
Description: First edition. | New York : Random House, [2018] |
Series: Welcome to Wonderland ; #3 | Summary: In order to
save the reputation of the Wonderland, P.T. and Gloria must
find the culprit who stole a royal tiara from the hotel.
Identifiers: LCCN 2016050421 | ISBN 978-1-5247-1758-2 (hardcover) |
ISBN 978-1-5247-1761-2 (hardcover library binding) |
ISBN 978-1-5247-1760-5 (ebook)
Subjects: | CYAC: Mystery and detective stories. |
Hotels, motels, etc.—Fiction.
Classification: LCC PZ7.G7487 San 2018 | DDC [Fic]—dc23

Printed in the United States of America
10 9 8 7 6 5 4 3 2 1
First Edition

Welcome to WONDERLAND

SANDAPALOOZA SHAKE-UP

Coming Attractions

"To tell you the truth, I don't know how I survived the fourteen-story plunge," I told my audience.

They were all sipping frosty fruit drinks and nibbling conch fritters at our motel's brand-new poolside restaurant—the Banana Shack.

"I slid over the first waterfall and rocketed into a ninety-degree zero-gravity free fall! It was a steeper drop than the Summit Plummet at Disney's Blizzard Beach!"

"Woo-hoo!" cried my grandpa, Walt Wilkie, when I mentioned outdoing his archrival, the Walt over in Orlando.

"I slid around an awesome loop-de-loop that shot me like a cannonball across the sky and into a log flume! Next came a series of wicked switchbacks, plus an aqua tunnel that hurled me straight through a tank swarming with live sharks!"

"That part was my idea," added my business-savvy best friend, Gloria Ortega, because *Shark Tank* is her favorite TV show.

"Finally," I said, putting the cherry on top of the ice-cream sundae of my story, "I splashed down in a surf pool, where I caught a wave and went boarding with an audio-animatronic Surf Monkey aqua-bot!"

"That is so cool!" said one of the kids at a nearby table.

He and his family were among the lucky guests who'd been able to book rooms at my family's St. Pete Beach motel after it became super famous in the movie *Beach Party Surf Monkey*—the Hollywood blockbuster starring Academy Award–winning actress Cassie McGinty, YouTube sensation Kevin the Monkey, and local hero Pinky Nelligan, who's one of my best buds. The "No" neon in our No Vacancy sign had been lit for so long we were afraid it might burn out.

"Where exactly is this waterslide?" asked the boy's mom.

"Right now, only in my computer."

"He used a RollerCoaster Tycoon expansion kit," explained Gloria.

"But," I said, gazing at the towering concrete hotel on the other side of our short stucco wall, "someday we might buy the place next door and actually build it."

"What?" said Grandpa. "All of a sudden you want to buy the Conch Reef Resort?"

"Hey," I said with a shrug, "it's the perfect height. Fourteen stories tall."

"Whoa, dude," said our new chef, Jimbo. "Are they, like, selling, man?"

Jimbo is what they call a Parrothead. That means he *loves* the laid-back, island-breezy music of Jimmy Buffett. Jimbo is extremely mellow and always wears a baggy Hawaiian shirt and sunglasses and has a ponytail sticking out the back of his baseball cap. He doesn't shave too often, either.

"Mr. Conch should sell his resort to somebody," I told Jimbo. "Because ever since our movie came out, nobody wants to stay over there except the people who wanted to stay over *here* and couldn't."

My audience laughed. Grandpa and I grinned.

Fact: Conch Enterprises, the company that tried to sabotage our motel's movie, wasn't doing so well anymore.

Double fact: Grandpa and I couldn't've been happier if all the doughnuts in the world were wrapped in bacon and dripping with cheese.

The Sweet Suite

"It doesn't get any better than this," said Gloria's dad, Mr. Ortega, who was hanging out in the lobby with my mom, waiting for our VIP guests to arrive.

"You're in the big leagues now, Wanda," he told Mom. "You just have to remember what got you to the dance, and focus on fundamentals."

Gloria's father, Manny Ortega, is a sportscaster on channel ten, WTSP—the local CBS station for Tampa, St. Petersburg, and Sarasota. He's changed stations a lot in his career. That means he and Gloria have moved around a lot, too. Since WTSP probably won't be Mr. Ortega's final destination, they're "extended stay" guests at the Wonderland. They rent a couple of rooms so they don't have to buy a house that they'd just have to sell when Mr. Ortega gets "the Call" from ESPN for his dream job.

Mom likes having Mr. Ortega at the motel. Me too. He's extremely cool. Mom and Mr. Ortega aren't exactly dating, but they do make goo-goo eyes at each other all the time.

What does my dad think about Mom flirting with Mr. Ortega?

Who knows?

My father, as you may have already noticed, isn't really in the picture. He hasn't been for twelve years—he left town before I was even born. Mom doesn't talk about him all that much. The only thing she's ever told me is "He was very handsome and very charming, and he could tell a good story, P.T. Just like you."

So, Dad, if you're reading this, drop by sometime. Apparently, we have a lot in common.

Anyhow, back to our big VIP guests. It was Thursday. After school. We were all waiting for the royal family to arrive. Well, not *the* royal family, but a family full of royalty from England.

They'd be staying in our one vacant room. Actually, it was a suite of rooms—225, 226, and 227— also known as the Cassie McGinty Suite. We call it that because that's where the movie star and her mom, a famous producer, stayed when they were filming *Beach Party Surf Monkey*. We even decorated the rooms with movie posters, stills from the shoot, and a few props, like Surf Monkey's boogie board and Cassie McGinty's framed hippie-girl costume.

Naturally, everybody wanted to sleep in that three-bedroom suite.

But that weekend, it was reserved for Lord and Lady Pettybone and their teenaged daughter, Lady Lilly. Lord Pettybone was a marquess, which is higher than an earl but lower than a duke, unless your Duke is a dog.

The Pettybone family would be traveling to Florida with their "trusted manservant" Digby, so he needed a room, too.

All in all, the royals were getting three of our best bedrooms because they were bringing us a ton more free publicity. The *Tampa Bay Times* had already done a big write-up about their visit. Sales of Royal Crown Cola were soaring all along St. Pete Beach. Even the St. Pete Beach Dairy Queen and Burger King were getting in on the act with "Our Royal Cousins" meal deals.

The royals coming to the Wonderland were traveling with the first Duchess of Twittleham's crown, which they called the Twittleham Tiara. Loaded with precious jewels, it was priceless and super special.

PRICELESS

OR IF YOU HAVE TO ASK, YOU CAN'T AFFORD IT.

In fact, according to legend, the diamonds in the Twittleham Tiara had once belonged to Queen Guinevere, King Arthur's wife in all those classic legends about the Knights of the Round Table. Some say Arthur got the idea for the shape of his table from Guinevere's crown, which was also round.

The Twittleham Tiara was worth so much money we probably should've booked it a room of its own!

Royal Treatment

"**W**e have a safe in the office," Mom said to Digby, the royal family's butler, who came into the lobby ahead of the others to make sure everything was "tickety-boo," which, I found out later, is British for "hunky-dory" or "okeydokey."

"I'm certain you do," said Digby, looking down his nose at Mom and sniffing like he smelled cat poop. The butler had a leather-covered lockbox handcuffed to his wrist. The box was about the size of, oh, a tiara. I wished I had X-ray vision. Then I could've seen all the Twittleham diamonds!

"However," Digby continued, "Lord and Lady Pettybone prefer to rely on our *own* tried, tested, and true security measures."

He tapped the box.

"It is constructed of two-inch-thick reinforced

steel and has a GPS tracking device embedded in its base."

"It's also chained to your arm," I said.

"Indeed," said Digby.

"Ah, you've met Digby, I take it?" said a man who walked into the lobby just then. He was wearing crisp white pants, an even crisper white shirt, and a posh blue blazer. An elegant lady in a billowy summer dress and a blond girl maybe a year or two older than me were with him.

"I'm Charles Pettybone, Marquess of Herferrshire," said the man. "This is my wife, Lady Annette Mary Gertrude Humphries Pettybone, and, of course, our daughter, Lady Lilly."

"Pleased to meet you," said Mom, doing a tiny curtsy.

"Meet me uptown!" said Mr. Ortega, raising his palm to slap our newest guest a high five.

Lord Pettybone left him hanging.

"I'm absolutely thrilled to be sleeping in the same room where Cassie McGinty once slept!" said Lady Lilly.

Her mother smiled. "Our daughter is quite a fan of your film about the surfing monkey. In fact, Lilly's insistence was the main reason we agreed to stop here in . . . Where are we again, Digby?"

"St. Petersburg, milady," said the butler, clicking his heels and bowing from the waist.

"Quite," said Lady Pettybone.

"Well," I said, "if you loved *Beach Party Surf Monkey*, you'll be happy to hear that the Wonderland offers all VIP guests an exclusive behind-the-scenes movie tour."

I showed Lady Lilly my elbow. "Recognize this?"

"Not really . . ."

"It was in the flick."

"Brilliant! So you're a movie star, too?"

"Nah. Just my elbow."

Gloria stepped forward and handed our new guests the glossy brochures she'd designed for our movie tours. Like I said, Gloria is an awesome entrepreneur.

"Tours start at fifteen dollars a person and include a stop at our Surf Monkey souvenir shop," she told our royal guests. "You can also enjoy a delicious Surf Monkey burger with curly monkey-tail fries at the Wonderland's all-new, all-fabulous Banana Shack."

"N'yes," said Lord Pettybone. "I'm certain we can."

"Plus," I said, "since this is a long holiday week-end here in the United States, St. Pete Beach is sponsoring its first-ever Sandapalooza sand sculpture competition."

"How fascinating," said Lady Pettybone, sounding

totally *not* fascinated. She turned to Mom. "Is everything as it should be with our arrangements?"

"Yes, Your Ladyship," said Mom. "I have you staying with us for five nights. You'll be upstairs in the Cassie McGinty Suite through Tuesday morning."

"I wish we could stay even longer," said Lilly. "Especially if there's going to be a Sandapalooza!"

"Lilly, love," said her mum (which is what they call moms over in England, I think), "we promised we'd take Great-Grandmama's tiara to Disney World."

"That is the main purpose of our trip," added Lilly's dad. "Won't it be thrilling to see the Twittleham Tiara on display inside Cinderella Castle?"

"Yes, Father," said Lady Lilly with a dainty bow.

We were glomming on to Disney World's big new princess promotional push. The first Duchess of Twittleham's tiara would be on exhibit in Orlando for the next twelve months. But since the Wonderland was the priceless tiara's first stop in Florida *and* this was the first time it had ever been in America, we had first dibs on all the hoopla and publicity, which made my grandfather very, very happy.

Having anything before Disney always did.

Walt Wilkie's Wonder World

Our family feud with Disney started way back on October 1, 1970, when my grandfather opened a wacky motel and miniature amusement park called Walt Wilkie's Wonder World.

It's why our motel grounds are still full of fiberglass statues of dinosaurs, pirates, spaceships, and whatever we decide to turn a refurbished Muffler Man statue from Michigan into. (Right now he's painted to be Ponce de León, the famous explorer—but we might turn him into King Arthur if Grandpa can find enough gold paint.) We also have our own Putt-Putt golf course.

Anyway, one year after Grandpa had his grand opening in St. Pete, another Walt had an even grander opening in Orlando: Walt *Disney*.

"We had one incredible year, P.T.," Grandpa always tells me. "One incredible year."

Walt Wilkie's Wonder World eventually turned into the Wonderland Motel, which for years barely made enough money to stay open. But then Hollywood came to town and filmed a movie at our motel, and—*KA-CHING!*—our money worries were over.

Of course, that doesn't mean *all* our troubles totally disappeared.

Because right after the royals checked in, our nasty neighbor, Mr. Edward Conch, the skeevy, not-so-nice real estate tycoon who owned the Conch Reef Resort next door, dropped by to pay us a visit.

Cheeseburgers in Paradise!

Mom, Grandpa, Gloria, and I were in the lobby, eating dinner.

Gloria's dad had already gone to work at WTSP.

The four of us were wolfing down Chef Jimbo's juicy and delicious Surf Monkey cheeseburgers, which are softball-sized globs of charbroiled sirloin smothered in melted cheese. Jimbo says, "I like mine with lettuce and tomato, Heinz 57, and French fried potatoes," because those are lyrics from a Jimmy Buffett song called "Cheeseburger in Paradise."

Anyway, we were all on our eighth paper napkin when Mr. Conch strutted through the front door and jangled our dangling bells.

"Where's your royalty?" he blurted.

"Upstairs," said Grandpa with a sly grin, "in our last three remaining rooms. How *you* doin', Ed?"

"Fine, fantastic. Never better, Walt, believe you me."

"Really?" said Grandpa. "I heard the only items on your breakfast buffet this morning were stale Cheerios and some kind of rubbery yellow goop you called scrambled eggs."

"That was the finest prefabricated egg-substitute product you can pour out of a cardboard carton, Walt. Cutting-edge, high-class, top-shelf stuff."

"*I* heard you're giving away free eye patches made out of construction paper and yarn," I said, piling on with Grandpa.

"Part of our Pirates on Parade celebration, Petey."

"It's P.T.," I reminded him. "Short for Phineas Taylor. Just like P. T. Barnum."

"My hero," said Grandpa. "The man who once declared, 'Without promotion, something terrible happens: nothing!'"

"Which," said Gloria, "seems to be exactly what's happening at your resort on a regular basis, Mr. Conch. Nothing!"

Gloria and I fist-bumped. "Booyah!"

"You guys . . . ," said Mom, shaking her head disappointedly.

We *were* kind of laying it on thick. Mostly

because Mr. Conch and his bratty daughter, Veronica, had tried so hard to ruin our movie shoot.

"Let me cut to the chase," said Mr. Conch. "As president of the St. Pete Beach Lodging Association, I'm here to remind you that this holiday weekend we're hosting our spectacular Sandapalooza sand sculpture competition. You signed up as a golden premiere sponsor. That means you get your own dedicated team of professional sand sculptors. You put them up in your motel; they sculpt whatever you ask them to down on your beach."

"Their room is ready," said Mom.

"And," said Gloria, "P.T. and I have already blue-skied several sand sculpture ideas we need to flesh out into actionable concepts."

Gloria knows how to talk in business buzzwords the way her dad knows how to speak sportscaster.

"Fine," said Mr. Conch. "Whatever. We're giving you the top team. Real pros, I kid you not. I personally handpicked them just for you. But before they can begin work, I need something else." He rubbed his fingertips together. "Your sponsorship check?"

"Of course," said Mom.

She found her checkbook and pen.

"How much do we owe?"

"Ten thousand dollars."

Mom wrote the check.

Wow.

Six months ago, ten thousand dollars would've been all the money in the world to the Wonderland. Today? It was just our entry fee for a sand sculpture contest.

Like I said, ever since the movie, things have changed in our little corner of paradise!

It's become even paradise-ier.

6

Free Advice for
Ten Thousand Dollars

Mr. Conch snatched Mom's check before the ink
was dry.

"Thank you for organizing this event, Edward,"
Mom said, because she's way nicer than the rest
of us.

"You're welcome, Wanda. If I were you, I'd be
thanking me, too. In fact, I thank myself for being
me every morning when I look in the mirror. Why?
Because I have a very big brain full of very big ideas."

"You also have a very big hotel," I sniped, "full of
very empty rooms."

"P.T.?" said Mom.

"Sorry."

"It's okay, kid," said Mr. Conch, hiking up his
plaid golf pants. "I have a thick skin. It's like rhino

hide. Sure, we've had a tough couple of months while you've been over here riding the Surf Donkey wave."

"Surf *Monkey*," said Grandpa.

Mr. Conch poked a pudgy finger in my face. "A little free advice, Petey? Be nice to the people you meet on the way up. They're the same people you're gonna meet on your way down."

"What if we take a different elevator?" I cracked.

"What if we never go down?" added Gloria.

"Oh, you will," said Mr. Conch. "Just ask the big shots at Pan Am, Woolworth's, and Blockbuster. What goes up must come down. That's why they invented gravity."

He headed out the door, tucking Mom's ten-thousand-dollar check into the back pocket of his golf pants.

"You guys," said Mom when Mr. Conch was gone, "you can't keep teasing Mr. Conch like that."

"Why not?" asked Grandpa, pounding a button on the soda machine and popping open his first can of Cel-Ray soda that day.

Yes, Dr. Brown's Cel-Ray soda tastes like celery.

Why anybody would want

to guzzle liquid vegetables with bubbles, I haven't a clue.

"After what those Conches tried to do to us, you want us to go easy on 'em?" said Grandpa, letting loose with a major-league burp. "Forget about it!"

"Why are we even helping the St. Pete Beach Lodging Association?" I asked. "We don't need a promotion like the Sandapalooza to boost sales. We're doing fine all by ourselves."

"Because, P.T., our neighbors—the nice ones—are like our family," said Mom.

"Um, no. You and Grandpa are like my family, because you *are* my family."

Grandpa dramatically pointed a finger toward the ceiling. "If I may quote Unknown—who is my favorite person to quote, because nobody ever knows if I'm quoting him correctly—family isn't always about blood relations. It's the people in your life who want you in theirs. The ones who would do anything just to see you smile. The ones who love you no matter what."

I stared at him.

"I suspect," said Gloria, "it's one of those things we'll both understand better when we grow up."

"Exactly!" said Mom.

"Fine," I said. "But right now, since we're paying 'em ten thousand dollars, we should hit the beach and meet our sand sculptors."

"You guys go ahead," said Mom. "I've got reservations to wrestle with. And Lord Pettybone wants lemon barley water in his minibar."

"Gross," I said.

"It's British," said Gloria.

"It's still gross."

Mom shrugged. "Most British food is."

The Sand Men

It was about six o'clock, and the sun was still hovering over the Gulf.

The sand sculptors had already started working on their creations up and down the beach. The "official" event would open the next day, on Friday afternoon, and continue through Saturday, Sunday, and Monday, which was a holiday. Prizes would be awarded Monday night.

There was a van parked on the beach behind the Wonderland. "Michelsandgelo Sand Sculptors" was painted across its side.

Two guys in cargo shorts and floppy sun hats were leaning on shovels and sniffing the aroma of Jimbo's flame-broiled burgers drifting along on the breeze. The taller one had a pair of binoculars and was using them to scope out the Banana Shack.

"Smells just like the juicy burgers I used to enjoy down in Bora-Bora," he said, lowering the binoculars. "Dee-licious."

"Gimme a break, Travis," said the stubbier one. "When were you in Bora-Bora?"

"When I was flying tourists back and forth to

the island from Tahiti. I piloted my own amphibious airplane, Darryl. What we call an island hopper. I used to land that bird right in the lagoon, putter up to the beach, and grab a cheeseburger at this little bistro run by a French chef named Monsieur Fromage."

The tall guy made me laugh. He definitely knew how to spin a story. In a weird way, he sort of reminded me of, well, me!

"Uh, hi!" I said. "I'm P. T. Wilkie. This is my grandfather, Walt Wilkie."

Grandpa belched. "Howdy."

"And this is my best friend and business partner, Gloria. We're from the Wonderland Motel—your official Sandapalooza sponsors."

"Gentlemen?" said Gloria. "We understand you two are tops in your field, so let's try to square this circle. When sculpting the Wonderland's exhibit, let's make sure we maximize our brand messaging by creating something linked to *Beach Party Surf Monkey* that'll do double duty as advertainment."

"You've been to college, haven't you, young lady?" said Travis with a charming grin. "I'm guessing business school. Do you have an MBA?"

"No, sir," said Gloria. "Not yet. I'm only twelve."

"Impossible," said Travis. "But for now, we need to put our sculpture ideas in the parking lot and circle back to our brand challenges offline."

"Kudos," said Gloria. "You used four clichés in one sentence."

Travis shrugged. "I like to read business books in the off-season."

"But we can't sculpt nothin' until our sand arrives," said his partner, Darryl.

"Huh?" I said, because we were standing on *the beach*. The last time I checked, it was full of sand.

Tool Talk

Turns out superstar sand sculpture pros like Travis and Darryl use something called heavy sand.

It has a different texture and is thicker than your everyday, ordinary beach sand. It'd probably be more annoying in your shoes, too.

"It's the same stuff they use for construction projects," Travis explained. "We ordered ours special from Carroll's Building Materials over on Thirteenth Avenue North. Mr. Conch wanted us to use cheaper, inferior material, like everybody else, but Carroll's is clean and soft, with no sharp shells."

"Travis and me are like postage stamps—first class, all the way," joked Darryl.

"Heavy sand molds better," explained Travis. "And it's a whole lot easier to shape with tools. Does your daddy let you use his tools, P.T.?"

"No," I replied.

Grandpa winced a little. He never likes it when people ask me stuff about my dad.

"P.T. can use my tools whenever he wants," said Grandpa.

"Actually," I said to Travis and Darryl, "I don't have a father. I mean, I do, but I've never met him."

"TMI," whispered Gloria out of the corner of her mouth. *"TMI!"*

She was right, of course. I didn't have to explain my father situation to two sand sculptors I'd just met. But for some reason, I wanted to. I'm not sure why. I guess they were just so easy to talk to. Especially Travis.

"Well, son," said Travis, placing his hand on my shoulder, "I'm sure wherever your daddy is, he still thinks about you. All the time."

"He'd probably let you use his tools, too," added Darryl.

"Sure he would," said Travis.

I nodded.

I also hoped it was true.

Metal Detectors
and Microscopes

Friday morning, Gloria and I headed back to Ponce de León Middle School.

"I heard from Pinky," I told her on the bus. "He's coming home from Hollywood tomorrow for a quick visit!"

"Fantastic," said Gloria. "We should work him into our backstage tour package. Have him autograph a few coconuts. Maybe name a sandwich after him at the Banana Shack."

"The Pinky Sandwich? What's in it? Bologna? Spam? Both?"

"Boom!" said Gloria. "Perfect!"

"Booyah!"

We slapped each other five. Fact: we make a very excellent team.

The second we walked into the school, our pal Jack Alberto told us he had a great new idea for a "big-time promotion" at the Wonderland.

Another fact: my friends love the Wonderland—and not just because we let them swim in the pool for free.

"Lay it on me," I said to Jack. "What's the big idea?"

"A metal-detector hunt!" said Jack. "You guys could bury something metal in the sand—like a watch or pirate doubloons or a toy truck—and then all the kids with metal detectors could comb the beach looking for it! Whoever finds it first wins a big prize!"

"Um, Jack—not many kids have metal detectors," I said as gently as I could.

"In fact," said Gloria, "metal-detector treasure hunting is typically a solitary hobby enjoyed mostly by males over the age of fifty."

"Sure," said Jack. "The old guys can compete. But I'll beat 'em! Why? Because I'm awesome. They call me the Ditch Twitcher!"

"Tell you what, Jack," I said. "We'll think about it. Add it to our promotional possibilities pool."

"You promise?"

"Totally. In fact, I'm thinking about it right now."

Mostly I was thinking that it wasn't such a great idea. But I didn't want to burst Jack's bubble.

Jack was still pumped about his metal-detector treasure hunt when we all had science with Ms. Carey. Science was the last class of the day. And Friday was the last day of the school week. Our three-day weekend was about to start!

"Before the switch is pushed to close the circuit and send electrical current through the school bell's electromagnetic coil, thereby causing the iron striker to be attracted to its magnetism and bang the bell . . ."

(That's how Ms. Carey says "Before the bell rings.")

". . . let me remind you that my virtual door is always open. If you have a question over this long holiday weekend, hit me up with an email, a tweet, or a text. Because science never takes a holiday!"

Maybe.

But kids sure do.

As soon as the bell rang, we raced out the door. It was time for three long days of fun in the sun!

Monkey See

When Gloria and I got back to the Wonderland, our beach was swarming with sand sculpture spectators.

"Our tram tours are going to be packed all weekend long, P.T.!" declared Grandpa. He was as giddy as a kindergartner. "And, Gloria? You're going to need extra sock monkeys in the souvenir shop!"

"Did the guys from Michelsandgelo create something to help drive sales?" asked Gloria.

"You bet! It's so amazing they shot off a few Roman candles when they finished!"

"Let's go check it out!" I said.

Gloria and I hurried down to the beach.

Travis and Darryl, our professional sand sculptors, had definitely done an amazing job. They'd created a wild scene with the Greek sea god Poseidon rising

out of a cresting wave with his trident to poke Surf
Monkey in the butt.

Awesome! It's like something out of a Percy Jackson book!

Or, you know, Greek mythology.

"You like?" asked Travis, who was putting on the finishing touches, smoothing out a few edges around Poseidon's crown with a bushy paintbrush.

"It's incredible," I said. "Reminds me of that classic Greek legend."

"The one where Poseidon chased the monkeys out of Greece?" said Travis.

"Exactly! First he opened all the monkey cages in the Greek zoos!"

"Because," added Travis, "the big guy loved to monkey around!"

"Correct!" I said, riffing off the story Travis was spinning. "And then he used his trident to poke all the monkeys in their butts and sent them surfing across the Mediterranean Sea to the beaches of North Africa. That's why there are so many more monkeys in Africa than in Greece these days."

"And why, many centuries later, the Greeks invented Trident gum," said Travis.

Gloria and I cracked up.

I heard a funny ringtone. Darryl reached into his cargo shorts and pulled out a phone that was chirping "La Cucaracha."

"Yello?" Darryl said to whoever was calling him. "Sorry, buddy. Wrong number." He slid the phone back into his pocket. "Dipstick must've butt-dialed me."

"Isn't it brilliant?" Lady Lilly came up behind us. "I got here when they were finished, right after they shot off the fireworks!"

"Those weren't really fireworks," said Darryl. "That'd be illegal without a permit. I just lit up a few Roman candles."

"They should've been *Greek* candles!" I joked.

Travis chuckled. "Good one, little buddy."

"Bravo, gentlemen," said Lady Lilly. "I feel quite confident that your marvelous sand sculpture is far superior to any of the marble statuary my mother, my father, and Digby saw on view at that dusty old museum downtown."

"Thank you," said Travis.

"I'm kind of hungry," said Darryl. "How about we take a break and go grab one of them burgers we've been smellin' since lunchtime?"

Suddenly, we heard a scream.

It came from our motel.

Up on the second floor.

Lilly's mother, Lady Pettybone, raced out of the Cassie McGinty Suite.

"Lilly!" she shouted from the balcony. "Thank goodness you're unharmed! Something ghastly has occurred."

"Mum? Whatever is the matter?"

"Someone stole the Twittleham Tiara!"

Trouble in Paradise

Lilly, Gloria, and I ran up the sloping sand toward our motel.

I texted Mom on the way:

TROUBLE! Royal suite. Someone stole 👑!

"This is dreadful!" cried Lilly as we raced past the poolside restaurant.

"Dudes?" shouted Jimbo. "What's up, man?"

He was coming out of his storage room with a big plastic bin filled with burger buns, pickle jars, and ketchup bottles.

"Um, minor emergency," I told him, putting on a smile and trying not to freak out the guests who were splashing around in the pool or wolfing down

Jimbo's food at the Banana Shack. "Don't worry. We can handle it."

We dashed around the pool and hit the staircase to the second floor. I saw Clara, our head housekeeper (and one of my favorite human beings ever), pushing her supply cart into the laundry room on the first floor.

"P.T.?" Mom tore around the corner from the front office. "What happened?"

"Someone stole Great-Grandmama's crown!" shrieked Lilly, who seemed to have totally blown that whole "Keep Calm and Carry On" thing the British are so famous for.

Mom clunked up the steel steps behind us.

Lord Pettybone met us outside room 227.

"Have you summoned the authorities?" he said the instant he saw me.

Oops. Guess I should've called 911 after I texted Mom.

"Yes," said Mom. "They're are on their way."

I looked around Lilly's dad and into the room.

The butler, Digby, was holding the lockbox, showing it to Lady Pettybone. A chain ending at an open handcuff dangled from its side. Its lid was up. The insides were cushioned with dark green velvet. Other than that, the box was empty.

"I had it chained through the ornate legs of that

I don't believe Disney World will be keen to display an empty box—although the green velvet is quite lovely.

iron table beside the sofa," Digby said to Her Lady-ship. "I just now unlocked the cuffs."

"Lilly?" said Lady Pettybone. "How could this have happened? Where were you?"

"Down on the beach. But I made certain that the tiara was secure before I left to take in the fire-works and sand sculpture displays."

"When was that?"

"Goodness, I'm not certain. An hour ago?"

"And you locked the door when you departed?"

"Positively."

"Of course she did," said Lord Pettybone, walk-ing over to pat Lilly on the head. He turned to his wife. "The door was locked when we returned from the art museum, was it not, dear?"

"Yes."

"Lilly would never jeopardize the safety of our most prized family heirloom, would you, dearest?"

"Of course not, Father," said Lilly.

"Did any of you give a room key to someone else?" asked Mom.

"Heavens, no," said Lord Pettybone.

"No one else has had access to this suite," added Lady Pettybone.

The butler cleared his throat. "Except, of course, if I may, the motel cleaning staff. In most establishments such as this one, I believe they have a master key to all the rooms."

Lord Pettybone snapped his fingers. "Yes! Of course. The maid. Who cleaned our room today, Ms. Wilkie?"

"I don't know if I would use the word *cleaned,* milord," sniffed Digby.

Mom ignored the butler. "I sent up my most trusted employee when you went out for breakfast this morning."

"And who, pray tell, is that?" demanded His Lordship.

"Our head housekeeper, Clara."

"Aha! We have our thief!"

Royal Pains in My Patootie

Clara was more than our best, most trusted, and favorite employee at the Wonderland.

She has always been like a second mom to me. Her family has been like my second family.

I remember the party we all threw around the pool when her daughter, Isabella, got into med school at the University of Florida. It was awesome. Even though Clara's daughter isn't a doctor yet, Grandpa calls her on a regular basis, especially when his lumbago is acting up.

"Look," I said, "let's not jump to conclusions. Let's just wait for the deputies to arrive."

"P.T.'s right," said Mom. "I'm sure there's a logical explanation. Perhaps you'd all be more comfortable waiting for them down in the lobby?"

"Actually," said Her Ladyship, "I'd be most

comfortable if our priceless tiara were still safely locked inside its box! What sort of establishment is this?"

"Ma'am, this room is now a crime scene," said Gloria, because I've sort of hooked her on a bunch of those CSI shows. We watch them together while her dad's working nights at the television station. "The forensic investigators will want to comb this suite for evidence."

"Very well," said Lord Pettybone. "We will await the arrival of the local constabulary in a more appropriate location."

"Um, is the constabulary the same thing as the police?" I asked.

"N'yes," said Lord Pettybone, inspecting me as if I were a gnat swimming in his tea.

"Do you know where this housekeeping person is?" asked his wife.

"Downstairs," said Mom. "In the laundry room."

"Do not allow her to leave the premises!" demanded His Lordship.

"Indeed," added the butler. "Your charwoman must be considered our prime suspect."

"Wait a second," I said. "Clara cleaned this room while you guys were out having breakfast, correct?"

"We went to the Pancake House," said Lilly. "The chocolate chips in my stack were absolutely smashing."

"And when you came back from breakfast, was the room clean? Were the beds made and the towels fresh?"

"N'yes," said Lord Pettybone with more of his snooty 'tude. "What, exactly, is your point, young man?"

"The tiara. Was it still locked in its box when you came back to the room after breakfast?"

"Heavens, yes," said the butler.

"Well," I said, "if the crown was still here *after* Clara cleaned your room, then she wasn't the one who stole it."

Gloria cleared her throat.

"What?" I said.

"She could've come back," Gloria whispered. "She has a master key."

Oh.

Right.

Forgot that part.

A One-Minute Mystery?

The royal family and their butler waited for the police downstairs at the Banana Shack.

They did not eat Jimbo's cheeseburgers, even though Mom said they'd be on the house.

"Unfortunately," said Lord Pettybone, "they would also be *in* our stomachs."

I really think His Lordship should change his name to Sir Snobbysnot.

I offered them sweet tea. With ice.

"Bad form," said His Lordship.

"Bad form, indeed," echoed his wife.

I had no idea what that meant.

"Here we are," said Digby, bringing over a pink teapot shaped like a flamingo that was usually one of Jimbo's goofy Banana Shack decorations. "A nice cuppa."

He poured the Pettybones each a cup of tea. Piping-hot tea.

Guess they didn't realize they were in Florida.

The three of them daintily sipped their tea (with their pinkies extended, of course) while Digby stood by, stiff as a cardboard tube, ready to refill their flamingo mugs.

Deputies from the Pinellas County Sheriff's Office finally arrived and took statements from Mom, Lord and Lady Pettybone, their daughter, and their butler.

"We'll want to talk to your head housekeeper," one of the deputies told Mom, mostly, I think, because Lord Pettybone swore he'd "have his badge" if the deputy didn't.

"Of course," said Mom.

"I'll find her," said Grandpa, "and bring her

around front to the lobby. You boys can chat with her there after you do your crime scene investigation *mishegoss*."

"Thanks, Walt," said the older of the two deputies.

Fact: Grandpa has lived on St. Pete Beach so long everybody knows him. They even understand him when he uses words like *mishegoss*, which is Yiddish for "foolish behavior."

"But before you gentlemen head upstairs," Grandpa continued, "I want you both to know something: Clara Rodriguez has been my employee and friend since 1992. Nicest person in the world. No way would she ever take anything out of a room except the trash bags and dirty linens. She is the hardest-working, most honest person I've ever met. She's even honest about Cel-Ray soda. She's forever telling me it tastes terrible."

"We all say that," I reminded him.

"But Clara said it first! I'll go find her."

Mom went to the lobby, probably so she could call our lawyer. I think we have one of those. Maybe not. We'd never really needed one before.

Gloria and I led the pair of deputies up to the second floor and room 227. I couldn't wait for the CSI van to show up with a team of forensic investigators. Maybe they'd even bring one of those dogs that can sniff stuff and lead you to the bad guy.

Or not.

Because while Gloria and I waited on the balcony, the two sheriff's deputies basically looked around for a couple of minutes, came out, and tugged on the doorknob to make sure it was locked.

"Did you find any clues?" I asked.

"Not really," said one.

"Did you dust for fingerprints?"

"No," said the other. "We don't really do that for missing items in motels."

"So, um, what do you do?" I asked.

"We file a report that the victim can send to their insurance company."

"You didn't find any unusual hairs or fabric fibers?" said Gloria.

"How about grass clippings?" I asked. "Grass clippings are good."

Both deputies sighed. "You kids watch those CSI shows?"

We nodded.

They looked at each other and rolled their eyes.

"I'm sorry to bug you guys," I said, "but Clara's my friend and this is my family's motel. I'd hate for something like this to hurt Clara or ruin our reputation."

"Did you offer to let those British people store their tiara in your safe?" asked the older deputy.

"Yes."

"And did they refuse to give their personal property to you for safekeeping?"

·50·

"Yes, sir."

"Then don't worry. This is a tourism state. Florida law protects operators of public lodging from liability when something disappears from a room."

"Really?" I said. "Even if it was a priceless antique that used to belong to King Arthur's wife?"

"The guy with the round table and the sword in the stone?" asked the younger deputy.

I nodded.

"Oooh. I'd like to have seen that. . . ."

"Look," said the older deputy, "even if you guys were negligent, your guest cannot recover more than one thousand dollars for jewelry or cash left with a hotel for safekeeping. It's a state law. So don't worry."

"Whew," I said. "That's a relief."

"But," said Gloria, "you still have to consider the business ramifications. A theft like this could seriously tarnish the Wonderland's brand image. This incident could turn into a public relations nightmare."

Gloria, of course, was right.

Fact: she usually is.

"We need to head downstairs and talk to Mrs. Rodriguez," said the older deputy. "If we don't, Lord What's-His-Name might challenge me to a duel."

Clearing Clara

"Hello, Marco," Clara said to the younger of the two deputies. "How's your mother?"

"Fine, thank you, Mrs. Rodriguez."

"Will I see you at church on Sunday?"

"I'm, uh, you know, thinking about it, ma'am."

"Bueno," said Clara, patting the deputy's folded hands.

We were seated around the linoleum table in our coffee room/business center. The two deputies were eyeing the nearly empty tray that held a few sliced-in-half doughnuts and crumbly coffee cake left over from our breakfast buffet. We're talking eight hours stale. Gloria, Grandpa, and I were at the table with Clara for moral support. Mom was in the lobby, covering the front desk.

"We need to ask you a few questions, Mrs. Rodriguez," said the older deputy.

"I understand."

"If you need legal advice," said Grandpa, "I'm right here."

Clara smiled. "Thank you, Walt."

"No problem." Grandpa burped. Again.

"So, uh, Mrs. Rodriguez," said the younger deputy, "did you steal anything out of that royal family's room today?"

She gave him a look. "What do you think, Marco?"

"I think you know that stealing is wrong."

"And who taught you that in Sunday school?"

"You did, ma'am."

"I rest my case," said Grandpa, taking a triumphant swig from his Cel-Ray can.

The sheriff's deputies asked Clara a few more questions. She showed them her clipboard with notes about what time she cleaned each room on her list.

"Thank you for your cooperation, Mrs. Rodriguez," said the older deputy. "That's all we need."

"But we still have to find out whodunit," I said.

"Not really. I'm sure our visiting royals have some pretty heavy-duty tiara insurance. The company will make a nice settlement." He glanced up at the sand-dollar wall clock. "Maybe we should all stay in here a little longer so Lord Petticoat doesn't give us any more grief."

"That's fine by me," said Clara with a small laugh.

"Would you boys like a sandwich while we wait?" asked Grandpa. "I could go whip up a few bologna-and-mustards on white bread."

Both deputies said, "No thanks." But they did help themselves to the leftover doughnuts. We sat around for fifteen minutes, talking about the Tampa Bay Rays' chances this season. Since Gloria's dad is a sportscaster, she knew more about the team and their stats than anybody else at the table.

●　●　●

Lord and Lady Pettybone were not happy when the deputies went out to the Banana Shack to tell them that they should file an insurance claim.

"Surely you're arresting the scullery maid!" said Lady Pettybone.

"No, ma'am," said Marco. "Her alibi checks out."

"This is completely unacceptable," fumed Lord Pettybone. "We must locate the Duchess of Twittle-ham's tiara. Its arrival is eagerly anticipated at Disney World!"

"I agree, Father," said Lady Lilly. "Mickey Mouse will be ever so disappointed."

That made me smile—but only on the inside. I

could picture the whole funny scene playing out in Orlando. A weeping Mickey. A crushed Cinderella.

I wasn't smiling so much on the inside *or* outside ten minutes later.

Digby marched into the lobby and demanded that we send up a bellhop as soon as it was "most convenient."

The royal family was checking out.

"However, they shall be remaining close by for several days to monitor the progress of this criminal investigation. If, by chance, your housekeeping staff should come to their senses and discover the missing tiara, please inform us immediately."

"Of course," said Mom. "Where will you be staying?"

"Next door," said Digby. "In the royal suite at the Conch Reef Resort."

Bellhopping to It

I, of course, was the bellhop on duty that night, so I had the great displeasure of going up to the Cassie McGinty Suite and piling the royal family's mountain of suitcases and trunks and makeup bags on a cart to push to the Conch Reef Resort.

At this point, you might be wondering how, exactly, I was planning to roll the cart down the staircase to the first floor.

I wasn't.

I was just going to load a baggage cart on the second floor, push it to the steps, unload the bags and carry them down the staircase two at a time, and then reload them all on our first-floor baggage wagon.

Good times.

"Deliver the luggage to the Conch Reef Resort,"

bellowed Digby, loudly enough for everybody enjoying Jimbo's burgers on the patio to hear.

Then he launched into what sounded like a speech from Shakespeare.

"And whilst in transit, do not dare steal anything else from Lord and Lady Pettybone! We have taken a strict inventory of all items secured in those several suitcases and will know immediately if you, bellboy, like your nefarious housekeeping staff, pilfer anything!"

Yep. Everybody downstairs heard *that* rant.

"The housekeeper stole something?" I heard somebody ask.

"Indeed she did!" said Digby dramatically, turning to address his rapt audience below.

"No she didn't!" I cried, but my voice didn't boom the way Digby's did. It sort of whined.

"The housekeeping staff in this establishment is a blight upon all those who nobly toil in service!" decreed the noble Digby.

He made a grand exit.

I pushed the wobbly cart.

As I jounced it along the balcony, I could hear the rumblings of a major panic bounce from café table to café table like a pinball trapped in the blinking bumpers.

"Did they fire the maid?"

"They should've."

"I'm missing a sock," said a woman.

"Me too!" said another.

"We found it in the dryer, Mom," said her son.

"That doesn't matter. If the staff is stealing things, I really don't want to stay here anymore!"

"But we've got to stay here," wailed a teenaged girl. "This is where they shot *Beach Party Surf Monkey*!"

"Is it?" said her dad. "Or are they lying about that, too?"

"Liars *and* thieves?" said a lady.

"Those jewel thief brothers stayed here!" said someone else. "Remember?"

"What's wrong with these people?"

You guessed it. Within an hour, half of our guests had trooped into the lobby, demanded refunds, and checked out.

Worse, a dozen of them had written about their "horrible experience" on the TripAdvisor website.

Gloria and Grandpa helped me bellhop everybody's luggage out to the parking lot and roll it next door to the Conch Reef Resort, which had plenty of empty rooms.

Of course, now the Wonderland did, too.

For the first time in months, Grandpa had to flick off the "No" neon in our No Vacancy sign.

16

Zombie Alert

The next morning, Saturday, the jumbo video screen in front of the Conch Reef Resort was flashing all sorts of "The Safest Rooms on St. Pete Beach" ads.

They'd even taken out radio ads boasting, "We're so safe we have safes in every room."

"Plus," the cheesy announcer promised, "unlike at some local motels, at the Conch Reef Resort, our maids go through a fourteen-point screening process. They're so honest many are former nuns or FBI agents. Some were both. Maybe that's why there hasn't been a reported room theft at the Conch Reef Resort since the day we opened, which is more than our neighbors can say. Especially our next-door neighbor. The small motel with all the goofy statues. We won't mention the motel's name, but it's a *wonder* they can *land* any guests at all."

"Can they legally say that?" I said to nobody in particular.

Gloria and I were sitting on stools at the Banana Shack counter, listening to Jimbo's radio, which, of course, was tuned to the station that played the most Jimmy Buffett songs.

"Doesn't matter if they *can* say it, man," said Jimbo. "They already did. The bad vibes have leaked into the ozone, dudes. Bummer."

"We need to go into heavy-duty damage-control mode ASAP," said Gloria. "If we don't spin this story our way soon, their version will gain traction and turn into a zombie."

I arched an eyebrow. "Huh?"

"We won't be able to kill it!"

"You know what, P.T.?" said Jimbo. "You should, like, go next door and politely ask Mr. Conch to, you know, chill. Tell him and his minions to stop saying mean stuff about your motel, man. Especially on the radio. He's ruining my groove."

Gloria and I both stared at him.

"Seriously?" said Gloria. "P.T. should go over there and ask Mr. Conch to play nice?"

"Yuh-huh. Totally."

Gloria shook her head. "Sorry, Jimbo. This is business, not nursery school. Nobody plays nice."

"Maybe it'll blow over," I said. "Next week, the royal family will be gone. They'll leave St. Pete Beach and head to Disney World."

"Without their priceless tiara?" said Gloria.

"Okay. Maybe they'll just head home."

"Without their priceless tiara?" said Jimbo.

It was like that was all anybody knew how to say that morning. Except for the radio.

"This just in," reported a newscaster. "Lord Pettybone, the visiting English marquess—which, by the way, is higher than an earl but lower than a duke—will be holding a press conference in fifteen minutes at the Conch Reef Resort to discuss his royal family's efforts to recover the stolen Twittleham Tiara, which was set to go on display at Walt Disney World early next week. The priceless diamond-and-pearl-studded tiara, said to have been worn by the legendary queen Guinevere, went missing at St. Pete Beach's famous, and now infamous, Wonderland Motel. . . ."

I snapped off Jimbo's radio. This wasn't the kind of publicity we'd been hoping for from the tiara.

"We need to go next door," I told Gloria. "There's a zombie on the loose over there!"

Mess Conference

As we hurried to the luxury resort—walking past our now-empty pool and our even emptier Banana Shack—I had a feeling that all the negative noise about the missing tiara might be able to do what evil bankers and conniving Conches couldn't.

This scandal could destroy the Wonderland.

When we hit the Conch Reef Resort lobby, Gloria's dad was already there, wearing his navy-blue WTSP blazer. So were about two dozen other reporters and camerapeople.

"Sorry, P.T.," said Mr. Ortega. "But channel ten needed someone to cover the impromptu press conference. And as the legendary ballplayer Yogi Berra once said, 'When you come to a fork in the road, take it!'"

"Dad?" said Gloria. "Go easy on the sports jargon. This is a *news* conference."

"Check. I'll keep my eye on the ball."

Mr. Conch and his annoying daughter, Veronica, hustled around the resort's mirror-lined lobby, passing out cardboard crowns they must've gotten from Burger King. Mr. Conch went to the podium and its cluster of microphones.

"Good morning, everybody," he said, pouting his lower lip. "My daughter, Veronica, and I wanted to personally give you a royal welcome to the most amazingly spectacular five-star resort complex in all of St. Pete Beach. People tell me all the time, 'Edward, you run the finest establishments anywhere, including Florida.' It's true. I do."

Tell them how awesome I am, too, Daddy!

I will, sweetie. Just as soon as I'm done talking about me.

That won't be till next week!

Finally, Lord Pettybone stepped up to the podium.

"Ladies and gentlemen," said His Lordship, "although we have solid suspicions about who it was that purloined our beloved Twittleham Tiara, I have prevailed upon the Pinellas County sheriff not to arrest our prime suspect. Not yet, anyway."

What? I thought. *He still wants to throw Clara behind bars?*

"If the chambermaid who stole our family's priceless heirloom shall return it to us by Monday, no questions will be asked. No charges will be pressed. However, should Mrs. Clara Rodriguez fail to take us up on this generous offer, rest assured she will be prosecuted to the fullest extent of the law!"

Lord Pettybone stepped away from the microphone.

Mr. Conch rushed in to take his place.

"And don't forget, ladies and gentlemen, that crooked maid works right next door at Walt Wilkie's Wonderland Motel, where there are always lies to be told and personal belongings to be stole!"

It was a lame rhyme, but it worked.

By noon, another dozen guests had checked out of the Wonderland.

Losing Our Appetites

"So what are you kids going to do now, man?" asked Jimbo, slapping a pair of burger patties on the grill for Gloria and me—his only customers.

"Well," I said, "I know what we *won't* be doing: giving any behind-the-scenes movie tours."

"Or selling more Surf Monkey merch," added Gloria.

"Or doing our Freddy the Frog bit," I said sadly. "Or hosting a metal-detector treasure hunt."

"We were going to do that?" said Gloria.

I shrugged. "If we did, at least Jack Alberto would be here. Maybe he'd bring his little brother Nate. We could sell them both a Sproke."

A Sproke was a soft drink Gloria and I had created with Jimbo's help at the Banana Shack. It was basically fountain Coke mixed with fountain Sprite.

You could also get an Orange Sproke or a Root Beer Sproke. Grandpa tried to mix Cel-Ray with Sprite once. The cup nearly exploded.

"You know what?" I said to Jimbo as he flipped our sizzling burgers and flames flared up their sides. "I'm not really hungry."

"Me neither," said Gloria.

"Dudes, just think how Clara must feel," said Jimbo, sliding our hamburgers off the grill. "I heard that press conference on my radio, man. Lord Bossypants tore into her something fierce. Totally uncool behavior, man. Dude needs to drink a little more Mello Yello, if you catch my drift."

(We didn't.)

"He'll probably keep going after Clara," said Gloria. "He currently controls the narrative."

"Huh?" I said, because Gloria had lost me.

"He's the one telling the story, P.T. Therefore, he's the one shaping the 'truth.'"

"Then we need to do something," I said.

"Such as?"

"We need to give this story a happy ending. We need to find the missing tiara and clear Clara's name. Come on."

"Where are we going?"

"Upstairs! We should investigate the scene of the crime!"

"Um, the sheriff's deputies already did," said Gloria.

"Yeah, but they don't watch half as many CSI shows as we do! I could tell."

"Good luck," said Jimbo. "If your investigation needs any, like, you know, food or beverage analysis, I'm here for you."

He thumped his chest and shot us a peace sign.

Gloria and I headed up to the second floor.

"I'll check the keyhole," I said when we reached the door to room 226.

Since we still use old-fashioned metal keys instead of snazzy plastic swipe cards, someone could've picked the lock to gain entry. If they had, maybe there'd be scratch marks.

I found scratches!

About a billion of them.

Because guests had been jabbing their keys at the poor lock for decades, and sometimes they missed. So there was no way of knowing for certain whether someone had used sharp tools to pop open the lock.

As head bellhop, I had a master key that would open any door in the motel. It was the same kind Clara and our other housekeepers had.

"We need to put together a list of all the maids who were working Friday," I said, slipping my key into the lock.

"You think one of them stole the tiara?" asked Gloria.

"No. But they all have master keys."

"So do you."

"Fine. We'll put me on the suspect list, too."

"Did you do it, P.T.?"

"No! Why would I want to wear a diamond tiara? It would give me hat hair."

We stepped into the empty suite of rooms.

"Any evidence was probably disturbed when the Pettybones packed up and left," said Gloria.

"True. But we should at least look around. This room was Lady Lilly's. Her parents were next door in 225. Digby, the butler, was in 227."

"Let's check out Digby's room first. He was the one in charge of the lockbox."

"Good idea!"

So we went into the butler's bedroom.

And guess what? We actually found something!

Making a Mountain
Out of an Anthill

"**E**wwww," said Gloria. "Gross."

There was a balled-up black sock on the floor. Gloria bent down to examine it.

"It smells like bad cheese."

"What's that next to it?" I asked.

"Um, sand."

"That could be a clue!"

"This is Florida, P.T. We're on the beach. There's sand everywhere. Digby probably got some on his shoes."

"But it's a pretty big pile. Like a miniature ant mound almost. Plus, does Digby, with his black suit and shiny shoes, strike you as the kind of dude who'd take long, leisurely strolls along the beach?"

"Not really."

"Hang on." I went to the dresser and took the plastic liner out of the ice bucket. Then I grabbed a Wonderland notepad off the bedside table and flicked its pages like a brush to sweep the sand sample into the evidence bag.

"Very CSI-ish," said Gloria as I sealed up the bag. "Props on that, P.T."

"Thank you, Gloria."

We looked around the rooms for a few more minutes and didn't really find anything.

Except, *ewwww,* Digby's other black sock.

We spent some time poking around the bedrooms, the bathrooms, and the dinette. The only other things we found were some of the driest, dustiest cookies we'd ever tasted. Something called digestives. In England, they call cookies "biscuits." Probably because they need gravy. Or at least some butter and jam.

It's like eating a sandbox!

"Can we please get out of here?" said Gloria after guzzling water straight out of the tap to wash away the taste of the cardboard-flavored cookies.

"Definitely. But first, let me stir-fry an idea in your think-wok."

Yes, sometimes I pick up on Gloria's business-wiz lingo. Especially the goofier stuff.

"Go for it," she replied.

"Who was the last person in the suite with the tiara?"

"Lady Lilly. Her mother, father, and butler had all gone downtown to the art museum."

"And Lilly said she was certain the tiara was secure in Digby's room when she left to go check out the sand sculpture competition."

"Do you think she stole it?"

"Not really. It's a family heirloom, so it's already hers. But she might be able to give us some more information."

"Excellent suggestion, P.T. Only one problem."

"What's that?"

"Well, to get that information, we'll have to talk to her. And I wouldn't be surprised if her parents told her not to talk to anyone from the Wonderland until we turn over the tiara."

"But," I countered, "Lilly would probably *love* to talk to two friends of Pinky Nelligan, star of her favorite surf monkey movie."

"Um, there's only one surf monkey movie, P.T."

"So far, Gloria. So far."

I pocketed my sand sample and we left the room, making sure the door was locked behind us.

"We might be able to tempt Lilly with a souvenir. Do we still have any of those autographed photos of Pinky?"

Gloria grinned. "A few."

Behind Enemy Lines

"**A**re you two here for the buffet?" sneered Veronica Conch when she saw us trying to sneak across the glitzy lobby of the Conch Reef Resort. "If so, help yourself to all the crow you can eat!"

"Thanks," I said. "But why, exactly, would anybody want to eat crow?"

"I believe it is an idiomatic expression," said Gloria. "To 'eat crow' means you must publicly admit a humiliating mistake or defeat."

Sometimes when I'm hanging out with Gloria, I wish I had a dictionary app on my phone.

"Thank you for that stupid definition, brainiac," said Veronica, propping a fist on her hip. "We also have humble pie for dessert."

"Well," I said, "I'm sure the humble pie is way

better than your key lime, which, last time I had it, tasted like lime shaving cream."

"Why are you even here?" Veronica demanded with an exasperated huff. "We're very busy right now, because everybody from your sad little motel just moved into our spectacular world-class luxury resort, and Daddy's making me put chocolate mints on everybody's pillows."

"That's just it," I said. "One of your new guests left some personal property over at our place."

"You mean the diamond tiara your housekeeper stole?"

"Clara didn't—"

Gloria raised her hand because she could tell I was about to explode. It would've made the shiny lobby messy.

"Lady Lilly left behind a treasured possession of her own," Gloria calmly explained, flapping the envelope we'd slipped Pinky's autographed glossy into.

"Give it to me," said Veronica, thrusting out her grubby chocolate-smeared hand. I think she'd been helping herself to a few of those pillow mints. "I'll take it to her."

"Actually," I said, "I can't do that."

"Why not?"

Since I didn't have a good answer, I made one up.

"Hotel Bellhop Code. Article fourteen, subsection C. 'Any and all articles entrusted to a bellhop must be delivered directly into the hands of those for whom they are intended without the use of intermediaries or ancillary agents.'"

"Well, how the heck am I supposed to know all that stuff?" whined Veronica. "I'm not a bellhop. We hire people to do that kind of junk for us. Too bad you guys can't hire anybody to do anything

anymore. Daddy says you're basically going out of business! Soon! Like this week."

"Have you seen Lady Lilly?" asked Gloria.

"She's at the pool. You can't miss her. She's wearing neon-green shorts."

"Thank you," I said.

"Whatever," said Veronica. Then she flicked her hand at us like we were flies she needed to shoo away from her potato salad.

We exited through the rear doors of the lobby and headed for the ginormous swimming pool, where a lot of guests I recognized from our pool were splashing around and having fun.

"There she is," said Gloria, pointing to a chaise lounge in the distance.

It was Lilly, all right. Her shorts were fluorescent green, like the reflective vests that road crews sometimes wear.

And believe it or not, she had on a sparkling crown!

It glinted in the sun whenever she moved her head.

"Wow," I said. "Maybe she *did* steal her own tiara!"

21

Princess for a Day

Gloria and I made our way around the pool.

I'd almost forgotten that the Conches had installed a towering poolside pirate statue to compete with all our fiberglass figurines.

As we approached Lady Lilly, her crown shot blinding beams of light straight into my eyeballs every time she jiggled her head. The thing was covered with bling. All those diamonds from Queen Guinevere were sparkling in the sunshine.

I started wondering if the whole reported theft was a publicity stunt, a headline-grabbing story to give the Twittleham Tiara a little extra sizzle and pizzazz. You know: *"Come see the royal tiara so super special it was almost stolen on its way to Disney World!"*

Grandpa taught me a long time ago that the

story is what sells an attraction. Stories are what make Disney World so popular. Why do so many parents plunk down thirty bucks for a stuffed snowman doll? Because the second their kids see his floppy carrot nose and googly eyes, they know it's Olaf from *Frozen* and they start singing his song.

It's not a plush toy; it's a story!

That's the big difference between the Conch's giant pirate statue and the Wonderland's life-size buccaneer, Stinky Beard, who stands guard at the entrance to our miniature golf course.

The Conch's pirate is just a hollow plastic shell.

Our Stinky Beard commemorates the smelliest pirate ever to sail the seven seas, because even with all that water, he never took a bath. They say his beard reeked of three-week-old fish chowder. That his toes smelled like last week's shrimp sitting in the sun.

In fact, Stinky Beard was so smelly his crew mutinied and left him stranded on the sands of St. Pete Beach, where he opened Florida's first miniature golf course right there at—you guessed it—the current site of the Wonderland.

At least that's the story I'd tell you to make playing miniature golf at the Wonderland a little more fun. And if somebody farted while I was telling my tall tale? Even better!

Gloria and I reached Lady Lilly's chair.

I had to shield my eyes from all the sparkly reflections.

"Looks like you found your tiara," I said.

"Have you gone absolutely doolally?" Lilly giggled. "You don't seriously think this crown is real, do you?"

Now that we were closer and Lilly was in the shade, I could tell her headpiece was a toy made out of plastic and rhinestones.

"I've simply been practicing my proper princess posture and poses. Mum insists I work with a crown for at least an hour every day. We must be prepared, mustn't we?"

"For what?" asked Gloria.

"For the day I become a real princess. In fact, I

might actually marry Prince George when he grows up. He's only a few years younger than me."

"A few?" said Gloria. "Try twelve."

"If we fall in love, a decade's difference in our ages won't matter! We're royals. Never forget, Catherine of Aragon was several years older than Henry the Eighth when they wed. All it will take is for dashing Prince George to see me across a crowded ballroom, sweep me off my feet, and make me his bride!"

"Sounds like a plan," I said.

"Quite. Now then, if I may, what brings you two over here to this much nicer hotel?"

"We wanted to give you a souvenir of your stay in the Cassie McGinty Suite," I said, sliding the autographed photo of Pinky Nelligan out of its envelope.

Good thing Lilly was sitting down.

"Oh my word! That's Pinky Nelligan! He's ever so dreamy!"

I held the photo away from her gimme-gimme hands.

"So, Lilly," I said, "where exactly was the Twittleham Tiara when you left the suite?"

"In Digby's room, of course. Locked up tight in its box, which was handcuffed to a sturdy iron table."

"Do you guys still have that lockbox?" asked Gloria.

"Of course. And now that we no longer possess the Twittleham Tiara, Mum let me borrow it for my practice crown."

She reached under her chair and pulled out the box. Its handcuff chain rattled and pinged against the sides of her chair.

I checked out the lock.

It wasn't scratched at all.

Cinderella's Sand Castle

Gloria and I puzzled over our new evidence as we hiked down to the beach behind the Conch Reef Resort.

"The box didn't look like it was forced open," I said. "Someone with a key had to unlock it."

"Or," said Gloria, "they had precision lock-picking tools and were experts at using them."

"True. So basically, we've got nothing?"

"Basically."

By taking the beach route back to the Wonderland, we not only avoided the Conch's lobby (and the possibility of bumping into Veronica again) but also ended up in the middle of the St. Pete Beach Sandapalooza. It felt like a carnival filled with sand creatures instead of rides and booths where you could pop balloons with darts.

There were food stalls with everything from cotton candy to ice cream and orange juice smoothies. This is Florida. Orange juice has to be a part of everything. It's a state law.

Everybody was having fun except Gloria and me, because we had a mystery to solve and no clues to solve it with.

We found Grandpa staring at a sand castle being attacked by a giant sand dragon.

Sand can put out a fire, so don't worry about the dragon, kids!

JUICE

"There's only one good thing about this whole mess," said Grandpa. "Since the Twit family's tiara is missing, Disney is going to miss out on a chance to make another bazillion bucks selling rhinestone knockoffs of it! They have too many princesses over there already. And who wants to ride around in a giant pumpkin carriage, anyway? It'd be like sitting in a rolling zucchini!"

Have I mentioned that Grandpa has major issues with Disney World ever since the whole "I opened my amusement park first and you nearly ran me out of business" thing happened back in the 1970s?

We left Grandpa and hurried up the beach with the crowd until we came to the Surf Monkey sculpture.

That particular patch of sand was mobbed.

Because supercool Travis was spinning his spiel and putting on an awesome show.

Showtime on the Beach

"This, ladies and gentlemen," Travis proclaimed, "is the crowning achievement of Michelsandgelo's sand-sculpting career. Surf Monkey is our statue of *David,* but with more clothes."

"Plus," I shouted, "his name is Kevin. From You-Tube. Michelangelo's *David* didn't have the Internet. He didn't even have basic cable."

The crowd cracked up.

Travis waved for me to join him in front of the sculpture. We were going to work the crowd together!

"And this guy with the pitchfork?" said Travis. "Why, he reminds me of my old boss. Always poking me in the butt about something!"

More laughter.

"Of course," I said, "Poseidon wasn't in the first

Beach Party Surf Monkey movie. But he might be in the sequel!"

"Woo-hoo!" shouted some kids in the crowd. I figured they were Rick Riordan fans.

For the next five minutes, Travis and I spun a story that made the creation behind us become something more than a cleverly molded lump of construction-grade sand.

Travis winked at some of the pretty ladies in the crowd. A couple winked back.

Fact: Travis might've been the most awesome adult I'd ever met (besides Mom and Grandpa, of course).

"That was fun, son," said Travis after our show ended with a big round of applause.

"You should hang out with us more often," said his partner, Darryl. "We're here till Monday."

"I'd like to," I said.

"But," said Gloria, "we're extremely busy."

"Doing what?" asked Darryl.

"Trying to crack the case of the missing tiara," I told him. "People are saying horrible stuff about our friend Clara."

"Ah, don't worry about it, son," said Travis. "It'll all blow over. Come Tuesday morning, all folks around here are going to be talking about is who won the big prize at the Sandapalooza closing ceremonies on Monday night."

"That'll be us," said Darryl.

"Let's hope so," said Travis. "I'd love to leave the trophy with you and your mom as a parting gift, P.T. After all, you're our sponsors. If we win, you win!"

"Have you competed in many of these contests?" asked Gloria.

"Tons," said Darryl.

"We were the top sand-sculpting team in all of Florida twelve years ago," said Travis. "But then, well, we had to leave. The heat down here was too much for us."

Darryl laughed when Travis said that. "Amen, brother!"

"We've mostly been working in California and the Carolinas," Travis continued. "Cooler climes. Bigger opportunities. Not so many *complications*—if you know what I mean."

When he said that, Travis shot me a wink.

The wink made me start wondering.

It also made me start doing some math.

I was twelve years old.

Travis said he'd left Florida twelve years ago.

Now, all of a sudden, he was back.

Was it just a coincidence?

Or had Travis seen *Beach Party Surf Monkey* and realized what he'd been missing back home in Florida for a dozen years?

Was Travis my father???

Dirty Laundry

"**W**ell," said Gloria, nodding sideways to let me know it was time for us to move on, "we have a crime to investigate."

"Chill, girl," said Travis. "R-E-L-A-X. Take time to smell the suntan lotion. It's Saturday. School's out. It's a long weekend. Even the sun is about to take a dip in the Gulf to cool off."

"And our friend's reputation is taking a huge hit in the media."

"Gloria's right," I told Travis. "We've got to go."

"You're a good man, P. T. Wilkie," said Travis. "And if you ever need to talk about anything—anything at all—I'm always here for you, son. Stay strong. Be cool."

"We'll certainly try," said Gloria. "Come on, P.T. Clara's probably done for the day. Let's go see what she has to say about all this before she takes off."

We trudged up the soft sand to the path of paver stones leading into our motel grounds. While we walked, I kept thinking about Travis. I remembered what Mom had said about my father: *He was very handsome, very charming, and he could tell a good story, P.T. Just like you.*

Travis was definitely handsome. He had dimples. I think girls like guys with dimples.

He was also extremely charming.

And he could absolutely tell a good story, just like me.

I didn't tell Gloria what I was thinking. She might think I'd gone all soft and goofy.

But I knew I'd talk with Mom later. Make sure she and Travis spent some quality time together. It might be just what Mom needed with all the craziness and checkouts.

Maybe Travis would even bring her roses and chocolate.

Maybe not.

This is Florida. Choco-late melts. Even those hol-low chocolate alligators they sell at the airport.

We found Clara in the laundry room, loading a

Help me. I'm turning into a swamp.

pile of towels into our jumbo washing machine. The pile was a lot smaller than usual. We were operating at about 50 percent capacity.

"Hi, Clara," I said. "How are you holding up?"

"As best as I can, P.T. It's been a long day. My neighbor, who is a lawyer, thinks I should sue His Lordship for slander. My daughter, the future doctor, says I should take deep breaths to keep my blood pressure down."

"Don't worry," I told her. "The police know you didn't do it."

"Why would I? Stealing is wrong. It would also be stupid. If something goes missing from a room, who is the first person everybody blames?"

"The cleaning staff," said Gloria.

"Exactly."

I flipped open a motel notepad I had decided I should start carrying once Gloria and I launched our investigation. "So what do you remember?"

"About what?"

"Cleaning the suite."

"Nothing unusual. The British guests were very neat and tidy."

"What about the tiara? Did you see the lockbox in the butler's room?"

"That would've been room 227," said Gloria.

"*Sí, sí, sí*. I saw the box. It was chained to the table. I saw the tiara, too."

Surprise Evidence

"Impossible," I said. "You couldn't've seen the tiara. It was locked inside its box."

Clara shook her head. "The box was open."

"No way."

"Way," said Clara.

She fished her phone out of her smock.

"I probably shouldn't've done this, but I wanted my daughter to see the tiara. It was so sparkly."

She showed us a photograph.

"Does your camera do time stamps?" asked Gloria.

"*Sí*. And GPS coordinates. This picture was

taken in the Wonderland Motel, 7000 Gulf Boulevard, at nine-twenty-three a.m. yesterday morning."

"While the Pettybones were off having breakfast at the Pancake House. Can you send that photo to me?"

"*Sí.* But why do you need it?"

"Because Gloria and I are going to clear your name, Clara."

When I said that, Clara—who doesn't show her emotions too often, not even when she's just discovered a poopy diaper surprise under a bed—hugged me.

"Um, like I said, Gloria's helping out, too." I grunted it, because Clara is a very strong hugger.

"*Ven acá!*" she said. "Come and get some of this." She wrapped her left arm around Gloria and her right around me.

And even though it was sort of hard to breathe, we all ended up in a pretty amazing group hug.

When we left the laundry room, it was twilight. I saw Travis crouched beneath a lamppost at the edge of the Banana Shack's seating area.

He must've brought up a couple of jumbo buckets of heavy sand, because while we were inside talking to Clara, he'd whipped up an incredible new sand sculpture. A dog. With his hind leg raised like he was peeing against the pole.

Jimbo and what few diners we had were cracking up.

"Good one, man!" said Jimbo. "Just don't let the health inspectors see him! I think that might be a serious violation, dude."

"What's his name?" I hollered across the patio.

"Mr. Pee-body," joked Travis. "And, son, he's all yours. Because every boy needs a dog."

He waved and disappeared into the darkness. I figured he was headed back to the beach to razzle-dazzle the Saturday evening crowds still cruising through the sculptures.

"That guy is so cool," I said.

"Yeah," said Gloria. "Handsome, too."

"Is he charming?"

"Huh?"

"I mean, does he remind you of me?"

"Who said you're charming?"

"My mother."

"Well, duh," said Gloria. "She's your mom. It's her job to say nice things about you. So where to next?"

"The lobby. I want to bring Mom up to speed on our investigation. We need to show her that photo Clara took."

"Somebody isn't telling the truth, P.T."

"I know. It's up to us to figure out who."

I also wanted to take Mom down to the beach. If Travis was my father, only one person in the world could tell me for sure: my mother!

But something stopped us from going into the lobby.

Make that *someone*.

Plunderland?

Veronica Conch was marching up and down the sidewalk in front of our motel, wearing a blinking sandwich board that advertised the Conch Reef Resort as a "high-security hotel."

"Check out while you can, people!" she hollered. "Join the royal family and enjoy the royal treatment next door at the Conch Reef Resort. Leave the Plunderland before the barbarians on the housekeeping staff pillage your room!"

I looked up to the second floor and saw some very nervous faces.

"Book two nights at the Conch Reef Resort and the third night is free," Veronica shouted. "Plus, you'll get a ten percent discount on pirate eye patches!"

My turn to shout. "They're made out of construction paper and yarn! Stay here and you can play Putt-Putt for free!"

While I was busy battling Veronica, a young couple scurried into the lobby. They banged the desk bell because Mom wasn't out front.

I couldn't waste any more time on Veronica. I hurried into the lobby. Gloria hurried after me.

"Hiya, folks!" I said before the man could bang the bell again. "Can I be of assistance?"

"Yes," he said. "We'd like to check out."

"Room 229," said the woman.

"Okeydokey," I said, slipping behind the counter and clacking a couple of computer keys. "Let me just call up your record. I see you were scheduled to be with us until next Friday."

"Well," said the woman, "given the, you know, theft . . ."

"You mean the *alleged* theft," said Gloria.

"We'd just like to leave," said the man. "Now."

"No problem," I said, thinking fast. "Of course, you'll miss the world premiere of Chef Jimbo's newest gourmet breakfast special. Actually, I wouldn't be surprised if the Food Network swung by to cover it. Jimbo's been on TV before."

That was totally true.

Once, when Mr. Ortega was doing a report about kitesurfing on St. Pete Beach, he shot a couple of scenes on the sand behind the Banana Shack. Jimbo was working that day. You could see him in the background. He even waved at the camera once.

"Your chef has been on TV?" said the woman.

"A couple times," I said, because the kitesurfing story on WTSP was a two-parter. Jimbo was in the background both times.

"What's his specialty?" asked the man.

"We're foodies," said the woman.

I thought fast and remembered a blurb about Skyway Jack's, a local landmark, that I'd read on the Food Network's website. I'm something of a foodie, too. Actually, I'm mostly an "eatie."

"Does Philadelphia scrapple sound interesting to you guys?" I asked.

"Ooh," said the woman. "What is it?"

"A fried patty of pork scraps and cornmeal that Jimbo serves with fried eggs and a side of home fries, because if you ask me, everything tastes better when it's fried. Candy bars, Twinkies, Thanksgiving turkeys . . ."

"He's serving this scrapple tomorrow?" asked the man.

"So I've heard," I said with a wink. "Jimbo doesn't really like to publicize his daily specials. It'd be a shame if he ran out before the Food Network crew showed up."

"On second thought," said the man, "we'd like to stay."

"At least through breakfast," said the woman.

"Great," I said. "And who knows what Jimbo might whip up for lunch?"

"Is he famous for that, too?"

"Well," I said, "you can't really become a celebrity chef if all you know how to cook is breakfast."

"Maybe we'll just stick to our original reservation," said the man.

"Great," I said. "And don't worry. The housekeeper didn't steal that tiara."

"No?" said the woman. "Who did?"

"Stay tuned," I said. "I guarantee the real culprit will be behind bars before the weekend is over."

"We have some very solid leads," added Gloria. "Now we just need to peanut-butter out the tasks that will close the loop."

"That means we're going to spread around the jobs," I said, translating.

The satisfied couple left the lobby and headed back upstairs.

"Well played, P.T.," said Gloria. "Well played."

"Thanks. You too!"

I wanted to stick out my tongue at Veronica Conch, who was still outside, parading up and down our sidewalk.

But we didn't have time.

Not even to drag Mom down to the beach to bump into Travis.

We needed to go find Grandpa and ask him to take us to the supermarket.

I just hoped they sold scrapple.

Scraps of Information

Grandpa drove us down to Publix.

"Scrapple?" he said. "Is that the board game with the letters? Who'd want to eat those little wooden squares? Did a family of beavers check in while I was napping?"

I explained that we wanted Jimbo to experiment with his breakfast specials.

"Scrapple," explained Gloria, who (of course) had done some quick research, "is a dish that was created by the thrifty Pennsylvania Dutch. When they made sausage, they used the leftover scraps to create scrapple."

Fortunately, the meat department at the supermarket had one package of Jones country-style scrapple. And it wasn't past its expiration date (if scrapple even has one).

Grandpa studied the ingredients list, which, I had to admit, would've made a vegetarian weep. "Oy. I'll tell you one thing: this scrapple is no bologna."

Breakfast meat secured, we just had to worry about getting Jimbo to serve it with fried eggs and potatoes for the couple in room 229.

● ● ●

We took the scrapple package back to the Banana Shack and stored it in the fridge.

"See you guys tomorrow," said Gloria. "I want to check on the business news."

"It's a holiday weekend," said Grandpa.

"The best time to do an unpressured market analysis," said Gloria. She headed up to her room.

I asked Grandpa if I could talk with him about something.

"Sure, sure."

We sat down on a concrete bench facing the Gulf of Mexico. The stars were sparkling in the sky, and

Somebody in Mexico is probably looking up at these same stars, wondering why they're flipped around the other way.

under the full moon, the surf looked like a field of rolling black trash bags fringed with white foam.

"So, Grandpa," I said, "I know you always say I should discuss this with Mom. . . ."

"Uh-oh," said Grandpa. "Do you want to talk about girls again?"

"No! My father. Did you ever meet him?"

"P.T., I really think—"

"And I really need to know."

Grandpa looked at me. I looked at him.

He blinked first.

"Nope," he said. "Sorry. I never met the fella. But, well, I hoped you'd never find out about this. . . ."

"What?"

"He and your mother were over in . . . She had a job at . . ."

"Where? Tell me!"

Grandpa put his fist to his stomach like he was feeling nauseous.

"Disney World!" He spat out the words. "The Magic Kingdom."

"You're kidding." I couldn't believe I'd never known that.

Grandpa shrugged. "What can I say? She was young. She was going through a rebellious stage. All kids do."

"Why didn't anybody ever tell me about this?"

"P.T., there are certain things we just don't

discuss in this family. For heaven's sake, P.T., she sold Mickey Mouse ears!"

"So she, uh, met my dad in Orlando?" I shivered a little, wondering if my father might've been a guy who dressed up like Goofy.

Grandpa put his hand on my knee. "Whoever your father was or is, wherever he came from, I don't really care. All I know is he gave me the greatest gift of my whole entire life. You!"

"Thanks, Grandpa. Because I've been sort of wondering . . ."

"And if you did come out of Disney World, then you're the best thing that ever happened there. The happiest place on earth? Fugghedaboutit. *We're* happy! What's Disney World got that we don't?"

"Um, a castle?"

"So? We're building a bunch of sand castles down on the beach."

"Disney also has princesses," I said.

"Princesses, schmincesses. Gloria could put on a sparkly gown."

"I don't think Gloria would ever—"

Suddenly, we heard tires squeal in the parking lot.

Somebody was leaving the Wonderland.

And they were in a huge hurry!

Getaway Minivan?

Grandpa and I jogged into the parking lot just in time to see a minivan swing out of our driveway and onto Gulf Boulevard.

When it passed under a streetlamp, I saw the lady sitting in the passenger seat and recognized her from earlier, in the lobby. She and her husband were the ones we'd convinced to stay at the Wonderland with the promise of scrapple.

Come back! Scrapple is the most interesting breakfast meat in the world!

SCREEEEEE

"Of course!" I said.

"Of . . . course . . . what?" said Grandpa between gasps for breath. He's kind of old. He doesn't jog on a regular basis.

"That's the couple from 229. They were just two doors down from the butler's room."

"So?"

"So we told them we were very close to solving the mystery of the missing tiara."

"Are we?"

"Not really. But now they're leaving in a huge hurry after they told me they wanted to stay so they could eat Jimbo's scrapple!"

"Maybe they Googled 'scrapple' and found out what that stuff's made of," said Grandpa. "It's worse than liverwurst."

"Or maybe they couldn't stand the heat, and they decided to hightail it out of town."

"No," said Grandpa, watching the minivan turn into the Conch Reef Resort. "It looks like they're just hightailing it next door."

Gloria clomped down from the second floor.

"What's going on, you guys?" she asked.

"The couple from 229," I said. "I think they stole the tiara. Looks like they're going to lie low and stash the loot next door."

Gloria arched an eyebrow. "Seriously?"

"Well, maybe. I mean, who checks out of one motel and into another at nine o'clock at night?"

"Um, people who, for whatever reason, are afraid their valuables might get stolen at motel number one?" said Gloria.

"We need to go investigate this!" I insisted.

She shrugged. "Fine."

"You're wasting your time," said Grandpa. "The butler did it!"

"Wha-hut?" I said.

"The butler always does it. Read a book. Watch a movie. Good night, you two. I'm going to bed."

Grandpa shuffled off to his workshop behind the pool.

"I'm calling 911!" I announced.

"Why?"

"That couple was two doors down from the crime scene. They heard we were *this close* to solving the mystery. They took off. Fast. Who squeals wheels in a minivan? That's very suspicious behavior!"

I Rest My Suitcase

I dialed 911 and we caught our first break.

A Pinellas County Sheriff's Office cruiser must've been just down the block. Ten seconds after I got off the phone, we saw its blue and red roof lights swirling as it pulled into the Conch complex and parked right behind the minivan.

"Awesome!" I said. "Come on. Let's go help the cops bust the perps!"

"P.T.?"

"Yeah?"

"You definitely watch too many police shows."

"Or just enough!"

Gloria and I ran next door.

When we got to the resort's covered entry-way out front, we overheard the sheriff's deputies explaining to the couple, "The 911 dispatcher just got a crazy call from some knucklehead who thinks you two might be caught up in this whole diamond-tiara-theft deal."

That knucklehead would be me.

Gloria and I hung back in the shadows.

"That's crazy," said the guy.

"We didn't steal anything!" added the lady.

"Would you like to search our bags?" offered the guy.

"We can't ask you to open them, sir," said the deputy.

"It's okay," said the lady. "We don't have anything to hide."

After a hasty search of the suitcases, the deputies apologized to the couple.

I guess the deputies didn't really care that the young couple had stolen several of our towels, a bath mat, and a half dozen tiny bottles of Wonderland hair goop.

Actually, they didn't have time to care.

Before they were even finished apologizing, the radio in their cruiser started squawking at them.

"Unit twelve, proceed to the Wonderland Motel. We have a report of another theft."

Phone Trouble

Gloria and I raced back to our motel.

This was turning into a very busy Saturday night!

We beat the sheriff's deputies, who blooped their siren a few times, pulled out of the Conch Reef driveway, cruised down Gulf Boulevard half a block, and, lights swirling again, pulled up to our front doors.

I saw Darryl, the sand sculptor, in the lobby. Mom was behind the front counter. Darryl didn't look happy.

Gloria and I followed the deputies into the lobby.

"Deputies!" said Darryl. "Man, oh man, am I glad to see you two!"

"What seems to be the problem, sir?" asked one deputy.

"The sticky-fingered maid stole my phone!" said Darryl.

"There aren't any housekeepers on duty right now," Mom explained. "They all went home hours ago."

"Doesn't matter," said Darryl. "My phone was in its charger. Now it's gone."

"When was the last time you saw your phone, sir?" asked the deputy.

"When Travis and I took a break in our room for lunch."

"And what time was that?"

"Around two o'clock. We both had one of those Surf Monkey burgers. Man, those things are delicious. You ever have one?"

"Yes, sir."

"We had us some curly fries on the side. And a fruit smoothie. Fruit smoothie was good."

"Why do you suspect the maid?"

"Because," said Darryl, "Travis and me left our dirty plates and napkins on the table in the kitchenette. When we knocked off for the night—about fifteen minutes ago—we went back up to our room for

the first time since lunch. While we were down at the beach all day, somebody cleaned up our burger mess and stole my phone right out of the charger!"

Mom assured Darryl and the deputies that the housekeeping staff wouldn't steal a guest's cell phone.

"Oh," said Darryl. "They just go for the diamond tiaras? My phone isn't good enough for them?"

"Look," said Mom, sounding worn out, "we'll buy you a new phone."

I cleared my throat. "Um, seriously, Mom?"

"Seriously."

"It's a good move, public relations–wise," Gloria whispered.

"Oh-kay . . ."

"It was the newest model," said Darryl. "The one they just came out with."

"I'm sure it was," said Mom.

That seemed to make Darryl happy, which made the deputies happy. Everybody left the lobby except Gloria, Mom, and me.

Mom sighed. It was even sadder than her usual sad sighs.

"I really hate making this call." She picked up the phone. "Clara? This is Wanda. We know none of this nonsense about the tiara is true. But until we get it sorted out, maybe it would be best if you didn't come to work tomorrow."

31

Late-Night Eavesdropping

Mom was so totally bummed out after calling Clara, I knew it was probably *the worst time ever* to share my Travis/Dad theory with her.

So I let it drop. For the time being, anyway.

Feeling down, Gloria and I slumped out of the lobby and headed to the Banana Shack, which Jimbo keeps open till eleven every night. He also makes a very fruity, very frothy Tropical Breeze milk shake. It's way better than a Sproke.

"We need to keep working the case," Gloria said as we walked, because that's what partners say to each other on cop shows. "So far, all we have is a warm bowl of nothing."

"And a stolen phone," I told her.

"Right. There's that."

The Banana Shack was lit by strings of colored

lights, including some that looked like pink flamingos. It was late, so not too many people were still at the restaurant.

But one very interesting character was perched on a barstool, chatting with Jimbo while sipping a Tropical Breeze milk shake. A paper umbrella speared through a pineapple slice, an orange wedge, and a cherry was sticking out of it.

Digby. The butler.

"What's he doing here?" I whispered to Gloria.

"Only one way to find out," she replied. "Eavesdrop."

Gloria and I slid into a pair of nearby seats at a table on the patio. We kept our backs to the bar but were close enough to hear whatever Digby had to say to Jimbo.

"So," Jimbo said to the butler, "do you have to take your dinner break this late every night, man?"

"Indeed. Lord Pettybone and his family can be quite demanding. I'm on call twenty-four-seven, as you Americans say."

"Bummer," said Jimbo. "They can, like, wake you up and make you go fetch stuff in the middle of the night?"

"Can and do," Digby said drily.

"So if they wanted a can of Pringles and some Twinkies at, like, midnight . . ."

"I'd run to the nearest convenience store."

"Man. I want a butler."

"As do I," said Digby.

"So," said Jimbo, "what's the pay like, man?"

"Wretchedly abysmal."

"Does that mean it's bad?"

"No, my good man. It means it is horrible."

Listening to Digby grumbling and grousing, I started wondering. Maybe Grandpa was right. Maybe the underpaid, underappreciated, and underfed (he was totally wolfing down his burger) butler really had done it!

Grilling More Than Burgers

I stood up from our table and sidled over to Digby's stool. Gloria shadowed me.

"Excuse me, my good man," I said, because I was trying to talk like Digby talked.

The butler turned around, saw who I was, and gave me a stink face.

"N'yes?" was all he said, but, wow, it sure sounded snooty.

"I want to show you something."

"Oh, joy."

"It's a photograph that a friend of mine, a certain motel housekeeper, snapped yesterday morning."

I showed him the picture Clara had forwarded to my phone.

"Recognize that tiara?"

"Of course. It is the missing Twittleham family heirloom."

"Notice anything unusual about the lockbox?" asked Gloria.

Digby peered at my phone screen. "Not particularly."

"It's not locked!" I told him.

"Kind of defeats the whole purpose of a lockbox, man," said Jimbo, wiping the bar with a towel. "I mean, if you're gonna have a lockbox, you oughta lock the box. Otherwise it's just, you know, a box-box. Know what I mean?"

Digby sighed. "Lady Lilly was supposed to close it when she was finished."

"Finished doing what?" I asked.

"Practicing," said Digby. "Lady Lilly loves putting on the tiara and pretending she's a princess. Her mother encourages her efforts. Proper posture and all that. Lady Lilly left it unlocked when we went out for our syrup-soaked pancake breakfast. I chided her about her negligence, but her father, His Lordship, instructed me to remember my position and whom it was I was addressing so harshly."

Digby sniffed.

"Whoa," said Jimbo. "I'm definitely glad that snooty dude isn't my boss."

"Indeed," said Digby. "However, when I was

called away to join Lord and Lady Pettybone on their excursion to the art museum, Lilly assured me she would, this time, take full responsibility for securing the tiara in its travel box."

"Do you think she did?" I asked.

"I cannot answer for Lady Lilly. However, I would not be surprised if, once again, she forgot to properly secure the lid. She has been somewhat distraught of late."

"Does that mean she's upset?" asked Jimbo.

"Quite. When she was told that the Twittleham Tiara would be residing at Disney World for a full year, she was positively apoplectic."

"Hang on, dude," said Jimbo, grabbing a napkin and a pen. "What does that one mean?"

"She was enraged. Furious. Irate."

"Whoa," said Jimbo. "That's a whole lot of angry, man. That's not healthy."

"Indeed," said the butler. "Lady Lilly didn't want to share those precious diamonds and pearls with anybody. Least of all Mickey Mouse."

Does Everybody Go to Orlando?

First thing the next morning, Gloria and I trooped over to the Conch Roof Resort, hoping to have another word with Lady Lilly.

We wanted to find out whether she'd left the room with the lockbox unlocked. We also wondered if maybe she took the tiara because, like Digby said, she didn't want to share it with anybody.

Maybe the princess had done it instead of the butler.

"The royal family isn't here right now," Veronica told us when we entered the lobby.

Veronica was hostessing the "brand-new" all-you-can-eat British Breakfast Buffet. They'd given their morning meal the Jolly Ole England treatment by adding scones, baked beans, something called bubble and squeak (I think it was mashed-up and fried leftover veggies), and English breakfast tea.

"Do you know when they might be back?" asked Gloria, way more politely than I would've.

"Later," said Mr. Conch when he strutted over to gloat at us. "They went to Orlando. Needed to talk to the folks at Disney about the tiara. So, Petey, do you think your maid will fork it over by tomorrow?"

"She doesn't have it!" I said.

"What? She already sold it?"

"Clara didn't steal the tiara, sir. In fact, we're very close to clearing her name. We have a few new suspects."

"Is that so?" said Mr. Conch. "What are you, some kind of junior detective?"

"Yes, sir. And a very good one."

Mr. Conch was kind of squinting at me, trying to see if what I said was true.

I didn't flinch. I wanted to wipe the smug smile off Mr. Conch's face.

It didn't work.

He gestured to the crowd swarming through his packed lobby. "Well, whoever stole the tiara, we've definitely stolen all *your* business. You people have no idea how to run a resort. But don't worry. We'll do something nice with your property when we take it over. I'm thinking asphalt. We could turn it into a first-class parking lot."

My face must've turned purple. I was about to go apoplectic—that word we learned from Digby. Gloria gently took me by the arm.

"Come on, P.T.," she said, nudging me away from what was about to turn into an ugly scene. "Like you said, the police need us to wrap up our investigation so they can apprehend the *real* culprit."

They didn't and we both knew it.

But Gloria is a good friend. What I really needed was to get away from anyone named Conch.

"Lilly and her family should be back from Orlando later in the day," said Gloria after we were off the Conch Reef property and on the beach. "We can talk to her then."

Since it was Sunday, the second full day of the Sandapalooza festival, the beach was packed. The sculptures were all pretty awesome, except the one created by the Conch Reef Resort's professional team.

They'd built an all-you-can-eat breakfast buffet, which never looks very appetizing when it's made out of sand. Plus the eggs, bacon, toast, pancakes, waffles, and OJ all had cartoony faces and Muppet eyes.

"That is so totally disgusting," said Gloria. "Who wants to eat food that's been smiling at you?"

I wasn't as completely grossed out as she was. Probably because I was distracted. Hearing that the Pettybones were at Disney World made me think about what Grandpa had said.

Orlando was where my mother had met my father.

"I need to go talk to Travis," I told Gloria. "Something Mom wants me to tell him."

"Cool. Meet you back at the Banana Shack? All of a sudden, I'm hungry for a breakfast *sand*wich. Get it?"

"Got it. Save me a Sproke."

She took off for the Wonderland. I wove my way through the throng and made it down to the sand statue of Surf Monkey and Poseidon.

Travis was pocketing his phone and getting set to mesmerize the crowd by spinning another tale in front of his masterpiece.

Seven Wonders of the Sandy World

"**W**hat people forget," Travis told his audience, "is that the Great Sphinx in Giza, Egypt, was the best-in-show winner at the first sand sculpture competition ever held."

The crowd laughed.

"It's true. But after all that work, not too many

Yo, Pharaoh. Where's the beach, dude?

?

tourists dropped by to check it out, because the pharaoh was a dummy who held his competition in the middle of a desert instead of on a beautiful beach like this one right here!"

The audience applauded when Travis ended his spiel. Some even dropped bills and coins into a kiddy sand bucket labeled "Tips."

One spectator wasn't so thrilled: Mr. Francis Frumpkes. My grumpy history teacher from school. His mother's house is just down the beach from the Wonderland.

"Young man, that story you just told was patently preposterous!" he fumed.

"Thanks," said Travis. "So's your comb-over."

Fact: Mr. Frumpkes wasn't fooling anyone into thinking he had hair by combing six greasy strands over the top of his otherwise bald dome.

"I'm going to report you to the WHA!" shouted Mr. Frumpkes.

"The whaaaa?" said Travis.

"The World History Association! They'll put an end to your fact-bending shenanigans, buster!"

Travis gave him a jaunty two-finger salute. "Looking forward to it, sir."

Mr. Frumpkes stomped away without even noticing that I was there or that I was smiling. (Mr. Grumpface wasn't exactly my favorite person on the planet.)

"Well, hey there, P.T.," Travis said when he saw me.

"Hey there. Where's Darryl?"

"Hang on."

Travis grabbed his binoculars off the back of a canvas fold-up chair and checked out the Wonderland.

"Yep. He's back at the Banana Shack, ordering us up a couple of breakfast burgers from that Parrothead Jimbo. We can't get enough of those things." He lowered the binoculars. "Can I ask you a question, P.T.?"

"Sure!"

"Have you known your cook very long?"

"Jimbo? Not really. He's only been with us for a month or so."

"Huh" was all Travis said about that.

"Sorry about Darryl's phone."

Travis nodded. "He thinks the maid stole it."

"She didn't, because she wouldn't."

"I'll take your word for it, son," Travis said with a smile. "I'm sure it'll turn up."

"Me too." It was time to pop the question. "So, Travis, have you ever worked over in Orlando?"

"Sure, sure. In fact, if I remember correctly, my final Florida gig before this one was a Sandtastic Weekend—a big event over at the Walt Disney World Swan and Dolphin Resort. It was something!

They had all sorts of food trucks and a DJ Dance in the Sand Party. Lot of pretty girls came to the dance. . . ."

"And, uh, when was this, uh, dance and stuff?"

"Gosh, guess it had to be twelve, thirteen years ago."

I tried not to let him see how excited I was.

Twelve or thirteen years ago was exactly when Mom was working at Disney World!

"Did you, uh, meet any *special* girls when you were at Disney World?" I asked.

Travis grinned. "A few, son. A few."

"Stay right here."

Travis laughed. "What?"

"Don't go away. There's someone I want you to meet."

Travis threw open his arms. "No problemo. I'm here all day."

I took off running.

"Where are you going?" hollered Gloria when I raced across the Banana Shack patio.

"The lobby! I gotta introduce Mom to Travis!"

Yep, that's what I said.

Even though I was pretty sure they'd already met—twelve or thirteen years ago!

35

Checking Out

I nearly ripped the door off its hinges as I burst into the lobby.

"Mom? Mom? You've got to see something!"

"Give me a minute, hon," she said.

She had a long line of guests at the front counter—all of them, apparently, waiting to check out. I heard

one of them mutter, "Now they're stealing cell phones out of people's rooms!"

"I assure you, Mr. and Mrs. de las Heras," Mom told the parents at the head of the line, "your valuables are completely safe here at the Wonderland. There's really no need for you to cut short your stay."

The mother covered her son's ears. The father took care of the daughter.

"Well, what about the M-A-I-D who stole the T-I-A-R-A and the I-P-H-O-N-E?"

"Those are just unsubstantiated accusations," said Mom, who looked totally frazzled.

"Well," said the father, "people wouldn't be making accusations, unsubstantiated or otherwise, if there was nobody to accuse!"

"Huh?" said Mom. "That doesn't really make sense. . . ."

"Just give us our refund," fumed the mother. "The kids want to go swimming."

"And the Conch Reef Resort has an incredible pool," added the dad. "You should see the waterslide!"

"We're starting a special stay-two-nights-and-the-third-one-is-free promotion," Mom said with a smile.

"No thanks," said the man.

"That includes a free breakfast."

"No. Thanks."

Mom printed out their final bill.

And then she checked out the next two families waiting their turn to flee the premises.

"Have fun in the sun," Mom said sort of limply when the last of our early checkouts raced out the door so they could head over to the Conch Reef Resort and jump in their pool.

She turned to me. "Now, what is it you wanted me to see, P.T.?"

"The sand sculptures!"

"Seriously?"

"They're awesome. Hey, have you even met our sand-sculpting team?"

"Yes, P.T. I met Darryl. Last night. When he came in to tell me Clara had stolen his phone. Remember?"

"What about his partner? Travis?"

I was hoping the name Travis might ring a twelve-year-old bell.

"Sorry," said Mom. "I haven't had a chance. I'm sure I'll bump into him before the weekend is over. Now, if you'll excuse me, I need to go clean some rooms."

"Wha-hut?"

"I asked Clara to stay home today because I didn't want people staring at her or saying mean things. Now none of the other maids will clean rooms unless Grandpa or I go in with them. They don't want to be falsely accused of theft, too."

"But I think checking out the sand sculptures would cheer you up."

"No, P.T. What would cheer me up is somebody finding that blasted tiara!"

Mom practically clomped out of the room.

I don't think I'd ever seen her look so frustrated. I thought back to when the Conches wanted to buy us out, before we landed the *Beach Party Surf Monkey* movie. Mom wanted to take the money Mr. Conch offered her and move to Arizona. Retire while she was still young. I talked her out of it. I was guessing she probably wished she hadn't listened to me.

Gloria came into the lobby.

"I just saw your mom," she said. "What's going on?"

"We're losing even more business," I told her. "And the housekeepers are all afraid to do their jobs. We need to find that tiara, Gloria. Soon."

"We might have a lead."

"Really?"

"Dad just texted me. I think he has some new evidence!"

Instant Replay

"It's the bottom of the ninth, the bases are loaded, I'm three and two at the plate," said Mr. Ortega when Gloria and I joined him in room 234. "Do I choke or do I drive in the winning run?"

"Dad," said Gloria, "what are you talking about?"

Mr. Ortega wiggle-waggled his phone.

He smiled his ultrabright smile.

Then he jiggled his phone some more.

Gloria rolled her eyes. "Dad, can you puh-leeze just tell us what's on your phone?"

"Proof that Clara didn't do it but somebody else sure might've!"

"What've you got?" I asked.

Mr. Ortega shook his phone. Again.

"Friday," he said, "before the burglary was reported, I was out on the balcony, putting together an audition clip to let the folks at WTSP know I can handle breaking news as well as sports. Then real news broke and the coach sent me in. The news director had me cover the royal press conference on Saturday, which, by the way, I totally aced."

He raised his palm, so I slapped him five.

"Anyway, there was no longer any need for an audition piece, so I forgot about the clip I'd recorded until just now, when I was trying to free up some memory."

He put the phone down on the coffee table.

"See, I had propped the phone on the balcony railing and switched the camera to selfie mode. Then I backed up and launched into a piece about Lord and Lady Pettybone arriving in St. Pete Beach with the fabled Twittleham Tiara.

"Watch closely," said Mr. Ortega, muting the sound so we could concentrate on the visuals. "I never saw what was going on behind me, because, well, it was going on behind me! Here it comes."

We focused on the screen.

Jimbo, our chef, marched up the balcony behind Mr. Ortega. He balanced a tray topped with a stack of room service food under warmer domes. Behind him, a bright green blur rushed out of the frame.

While Mr. Ortega yammered at the camera, Jimbo banged on the door to room 227.

"That's the butler's room," I said.

"That's where the tiara was!" added Gloria.

On-screen, no one answered Jimbo's knock.

So he set down his tray on one of the white plastic lawn chairs outside the door.

He started jiggling the knob.

He knocked one more time.

Jiggled the knob. Harder.

He looked over his shoulder to see if anyone was watching him.

I couldn't believe what I was seeing.

Jimbo reached into his pocket just as Mr. Ortega finished his audition, stepped forward, blocked the lens, and shut off the video camera.

So we didn't get to see the most important part of the clip: Jimbo breaking into the butler's room to steal the tiara!

Fatherly Advice

"Jimbo did it?" I said out loud.

"So it would seem," said Mr. Ortega. "This could be the break this team needs. I've seen your mom, P.T. She's been struggling. She needs a win to stop this skid. And the Wonderland? It's about to slide into the cellar of the motel league."

"Dad?" said Gloria. "This is news, not sports, remember?"

"Check."

Gloria turned to me. "What do you guys know about Jimbo, anyway?"

I shrugged. "He's a nice guy who makes a mean burger and very tasty curly fries."

"What's his background?" asked Mr. Ortega.

"I'm not sure. He was a cook in the army. . . ."

"Or so he says, P.T.," said Mr. Ortega skeptically. "Or so he says."

"Let me put this on the stoop and see if the cat licks it up," said Gloria. "Here's my theory: Jimbo's had his eye on room 227 ever since the royals checked in. Don't forget, he can see who's coming and going in and out of the second-floor rooms from his post at the Banana Shack."

Mr. Ortega nodded. "I sometimes wave at him when I'm on the balcony working on my tan. Always wear sunscreen, kids."

"So let's look at this from ten thousand feet," said Gloria. "Jimbo waited until he knew everybody was out of the Cassie McGinty Suite. The adults went to the art museum. Lady Lilly scampered down to the beach when Travis and Darryl shot off Roman candles to open their Sandapalooza exhibit. Once she was gone, Jimbo faked like he was making a room service delivery and used a master key to sneak into the butler's room!"

"Jimbo doesn't have a master key," I pointed out. "Just the maids. And me."

"He could've 'borrowed' one," suggested Gloria. "He could've borrowed it weeks ago and had a duplicate made. We should call the police. ASAP."

"No. Not just yet. Jimbo's a good guy."

"So what *do* you want to do?" asked Gloria.

"Wait until there's one second left on the shot clock?" added her dad.

"Just give me five minutes, you guys. I want to talk this over with somebody. I think I need some fatherly advice."

"Um, this is my father," said Gloria. "And he just gave you some very sound advice."

"Thank you, Gloria. P.T.? Call the police."

"I will," I said. "Probably. I just want to check in with one more person."

"Of course you do," said Mr. Ortega, clapping me on the shoulder. "But remember, P.T.: a win today snaps your family out of this losing streak! Now go talk to your grandfather. See what he says."

"Yes, sir."

I dashed out of the room.

I definitely needed to have a father-son-type chat with someone else before calling the sheriff's office and pointing a finger at Jimbo.

But I didn't want to have it with Grandpa.

I wanted to have it with Travis.

What Would Travis Do?

"**W**ell, son, I'd say you're stuck between a rock and a hard place."

Travis and I were sitting in the shade behind the Surf Monkey sculpture. It was just him and me. Darryl was out front, chatting with the crowd.

So do you always have sand in your undershorts?

Yep. It's our number one job hazard.

"I'm not one hundred percent positive that Jimbo did it," I said. "The video ends before you actually see him bust in or steal anything."

"Well, the good news is you don't have to be sure," said Travis. "You can just turn this video you found over to the sheriff's office. Let *them* investigate it."

"But Jimbo's such a great guy. . . ."

"I know you like the cook," said Travis. "And I definitely love his burgers. But for the sake of your family, if your cook is a crook, he needs to go to jail."

I nodded.

"The sooner you make the call, the better, son. I've seen all those people checking out. If you don't move fast, there won't be anybody staying at the Wonderland except you, me, and Darryl."

"And Grandpa," I said. "And my mom. Have you bumped into her yet?"

"No. Not on this show."

"What do you mean?"

"Well, P.T., I've been doing sand-sculpting festivals for over twenty years now. You meet a lot of interesting folks along the way. I might've met your mom on a gig and not even remember it."

"She was in Orlando when you were there! Twelve or thirteen years ago."

"Is that so?"

"Yep. You might've met her at that Sandtastic Weekend dealio. She was working at Walt Disney World back then."

Travis grinned. "So tell me, P.T.—is your mom pretty?"

"I guess. I mean, I think so."

"Well, then," said Travis with a wink, "chances are we probably *did* meet over in Orlando. I'm not one to let a pretty lady pass me by."

I knew it!

This guy had to be my dad.

But he didn't want to come right out and say it. He needed to work up to it. I could respect that.

"So you definitely think I should call the cops?" I said. "Give them Mr. Ortega's evidence?"

"What have you got to lose? Except a few more motel guests if you *don't* make the call."

"But I feel so bad. . . ."

"You've got to do what's right for your family, son, no matter how it makes you feel. Family should always come first—before anything else in the world."

"You're right. Thanks, Travis."

"Anytime, P.T. Anytime."

We stood up, dusted off our shorts, and shook hands.

"Go get 'em . . . son."

Jimbo in Hot Water

I went to grab Gloria and her dad.

Together, we flew into the lobby to deliver our news.

"We have our burglar!" I announced to Mom and Grandpa, who were taping a ginormous banner in the front windows: "Stay 2 Nights and the 3rd Night Is Free!"

I think that's what it said. I had to read it backward.

"You guys?" I said, because they wouldn't stop fiddling with their sign. "This is super important! Clara's in the clear!"

"Hold your horses, P.T.," said Grandpa. "I need more duct tape over here, Wanda."

Mom tore some off the roll with her teeth.

When the hand-lettered roll banner was (finally)

Free! The most powerful word in advertising!

crookedly anchored in place, Mom and Grandpa turned around to see what all the fuss was about.

That was when Mom saw that Gloria and Mr. Ortega were with me.

"Oh, hi, Manny. I didn't know you were with the kids." She tried to quickly pat down her frizzled hair. And tuck in her blouse. And smile.

"Wanda," said Mr. Ortega, striding forward with his phone, "we knew this wouldn't be a cakewalk, but it looks like we're going to eke out a win!"

"Oh-kay," said Mom. "I'm not sure what you're saying. . . ."

"Jimbo did it!" I blurted.

"Huh?" said Mom and Grandpa.

"Let's go to the videotape," said Mr. Ortega, "even though it's really digits, not tape."

"Correct," said Gloria.

Mom and Grandpa watched the clip of Jimbo banging on the butler's door, looking around suspiciously, and digging into his pocket for what we all knew had to be a master key.

"He looks pretty hinky," said Grandpa.

Mr. Ortega arched an eyebrow. "Hinky?"

"Shifty. Strange. Hinky!"

"It's a black-and-white-detective-movie word," I explained.

"Gotcha," said Mr. Ortega.

"Look, you guys," said Mom, "Jimbo didn't do it. This video doesn't really prove anything."

"Um, yes it does," I said. "It proves Jimbo really wanted to get into that room."

"Probably because he knew there was a priceless tiara inside it," added Gloria.

"Maybe," said Mom. "But I don't think Jimbo would do something like this. And what if you're wrong? We could ruin Jimbo's life."

"Jimbo," I said, shaking my head. "Exactly what kind of name is that?"

"Sounds like an alias to me," said Gloria. "A

name someone who didn't want you knowing their real name would use."

"Or their real police record!" added Grandpa.

"The video is pretty solid evidence," said Mr. Ortega.

Mom was still hesitating. "I don't know. . . ."

So I pulled out my heavy artillery: all that stuff Travis had said to *me*.

"We've got to do what's right for our family, Mom. What if our cook is also a crook? Just let the deputies see what you saw."

"It couldn't hurt," said Grandpa.

So we called the cops.

Case Closed

The Pinellas County Sheriff's Office sent over yet another patrol car.

"You folks have new evidence?" asked the lead deputy.

"Maybe," said Mom.

"Good. We've been getting a lot of grief in the media about not solving this case."

"Not from me," said Mr. Ortega.

"You're the sports guy," the deputy said with a smile.

"Weeknights at eleven," said Mr. Ortega. "But I'm also moving into breaking news. This just in . . ."

He handed the deputies his phone.

They checked out the video.

Then they went out back to the Banana Shack to have a word with Jimbo.

Jimbo looked totally bummed.

"Deputies," he said in a soft voice, "I can so totally explain. . . ."

He was interrupted by a nearby phone chirping "La Cucaracha."

"Hey!" cried Darryl, who just happened to be standing at the poolside vending machine, buying himself a cold drink. "That's my phone!"

He hurried over to where the deputy was talking to Jimbo.

Jimbo dug through a pile of red napkins in a plastic basket that was sitting on the counter near some ketchup and mustard squeeze bottles. He pulled out the La Cucaracha-ing phone.

"Here you go, bro," said Jimbo, handing the phone to Darryl.

"*You* stole it!"

"What? No way, man . . ."

Darryl jammed the phone into his shorts. It stopped ringing.

"Arrest him!" Darryl shouted at the deputy. "He's a phone thief!"

"I didn't steal any—"

The deputy held up his hand. "Jimbo, how about we continue this conversation up in Largo? You might want to call your lawyer."

"I don't have a lawyer. . . ."

"Then we'll help you find one."

The sheriff's deputies put Jimbo in handcuffs and led him to their cruiser. They helped him duck into the backseat without bumping his head.

Why were the cops taking our chef to Largo?

Because that's where the Pinellas County Sheriff's Office keeps its jail cells.

Person of Interest

"The Pinellas County Sheriff's Office reports it is questioning a new person of interest in connection with the disappearance of the Twittleham Tiara at the Wonderland Motel on St. Pete Beach," said the radio newscaster.

Gloria and I were hanging out with Grandpa in his workshop behind the pool. We were huddled around his paint-splattered radio. Grandpa was duct-taping together a bunch of plastic garbage bags ripped at the seams. He had plans to rig up a home-made jumbo balloon to a leaf blower so we'd have our own wind-dancer puppet—you know, those floppy skinny things bopping in the breeze in front of used-car lots.

"Ours will say F-R-E-E," he'd told us. "That'll make folks slam on their brakes and pull in!"

We'll make his hair out of toilet paper and pray it doesn't rain.

"Lord Pettybone's family heirloom, however, has still not been recovered," the radio news continued. "As you might recall, His Lordship has promised not to press charges if the tiara is returned by tomorrow."

That was exactly what I hoped would happen. Jimbo would confess, turn in the tiara; he'd get out of jail free; and we'd all live happily ever after.

I was so glad I had taken Travis's advice and turned Jimbo in. I was also a little upset with myself for thinking Jimbo was such an awesome addition to the Wonderland team. Guess I'd let my stomach do my thinking for me.

"In other news," said the radio, *"Florida Fun in*

the Sun magazine has announced that it is gearing up for its annual Hottest Family Attraction in the Sunshine State contest. Walt Disney World has won for the past several years and—"

"Feh!" said Grandpa, snapping off the radio. "It's a rigged contest."

"No, it's not," I told him. "We have a shot. Don't forget, this is a famous movie location now!"

Grandpa shook his head. "Nope, nope, nope. Not anymore. Now it's just a motel where the cook or the maid will steal your family's treasured heirlooms and high-end cell phones."

"That's not true!"

"Doesn't matter," said Gloria. "Perception can quickly become reality."

"Yeppers," said Grandpa. "What Gloria said."

I was going to argue. Tell them that as soon as Jimbo returned the tiara to Lord Snootypants, everything at the Wonderland would go back to being like it used to be.

But Mom buzzed Grandpa on his walkie-talkie.

"Dad?"

"Yes?"

"Is P.T. with you? I need his help."

"He's here. Gloria, too."

"Good. I could sure use both of them."

Meet the Freebies

We had a crowd in the lobby, but it was more like a mob.

Some people were in a hurry to check out.

A bunch more—mostly rowdy-looking college-aged kids carrying coolers—were eager to check in. They'd seen that FREE banner in our front windows.

"What if we stay *six* nights?" asked a guy with blond dreadlocks and tattoos all over his arms, legs, and chest. "Do we get, like, *two* nights free?"

"Yes," said Mom, behind the counter.

"Great. Make those two free nights our first two nights. . . ."

"That's not how it works."

"Excuse me," said a man, covering his little daughter's eyes, because she was staring at the college guy's tattoos. A lot of them were skulls. With daggers in them. "We just need to check out!"

"You people got any food?" hollered a girl who was with the tattoo guy. "I'm starving."

"P.T.? Gloria?" said Mom when she looked up from the computer long enough to see us.

"Yeah?" I said. "How can we help?"

"This gentleman needs his bags taken to his car," she said. "He's checking out."

"Yo," said the tattoo guy. "We're checking in. We need baggage assistance, too."

"Sure," I said. "No problem, sir."

A family with what looked like a dozen kids between the ages of zero and twelve (three of them in what smelled like dirty diapers) marched into the lobby.

"We want one of those free rooms!" announced the clan's dad, pointing at the banner.

"Just one?" said Gloria. "There's fourteen of you." Gloria's very good with math.

"You're right. We're gonna need a rollaway bed, too. And a crib."

"Fine," said Mom. "We'll put you in the Cassie McGinty Suite. It has three rooms."

"But we're only going to pay for one!"

"Fine . . ."

"Hey," said the guy with all the tattoos. "We were here first. Give us the suite."

"Yeah," said his girlfriend. "Wait in line, bub."

"Suit yourself," said the man with all the squirming kids, one of whom kept cranking our gumball machine's handle to see if anything free would tumble out. "But the longer we wait, the more this lobby's gonna smell like baby poop."

"Do you folks sell diapers?" asked the mom.

"No," said Gloria.

"Well, toss me one of those souvenir T-shirts. This is an emergency."

"I just want to check out!" cried the other guy, taking his hands off his daughter's eyes so he could fan the foul air underneath his nose. "Please? Can we leave? I'm begging you. . . ."

"P.T.? Help everybody with their bags."

"On it!"

"And then," said Mom, "I need you guys to handle the Banana Shack."

"Huh?"

"I'm busy here," she explained. "Grandpa's helping clean rooms. I need to start the laundry. Jimbo's in jail. You two need to run the restaurant!"

"No problem," I said.

"Glad to pitch in, Ms. Wilkie," added Gloria.

She and I had watched a couple of episodes of *MasterChef Junior* on TV. Running our own restaurant might be fun.

"Is the food half price, too?" asked the mom, bouncing her squealing poopy-diapered baby in her arms.

Then again, maybe not.

Master Chef?

After everybody's suitcases were where they wanted them, Gloria and I headed to the Banana Shack.

We scrounged around in the pantry, found Jimbo's leftovers in the fridge, and checked out the ingredients we had on hand.

"So," I said, "remember that kid who won *MasterChef Junior* last season? The girl with the backward baseball cap?"

Gloria nodded. "Her appetizer was sake-marinated shrimp with a seaweed and sea-bean salad."

"Do you know how to cook any of that stuff?"

"Nope."

"Have you ever cooked anything?"

"Macaroni and cheese from a box."

"No worries," I said. "I know how to cook."

"Excellent, Chef," said Gloria, because on the TV show, everybody always calls each other Chef. "What do you know how to make?"

"Hot dogs. Grilled cheese. I can kind of do a burger."

"What about French fries?"

I gestured to a pan filled with precooked curly fries. "We're in luck. Jimbo already made a batch."

Gloria sampled a fry. "They're cold. He probably cooked these yesterday."

"So? If anybody orders fries, we can warm them up in the microwave."

The first customers to belly up to the Banana Shack bar were the tattooed dude and his "starving" girlfriend.

"Hey, kid?"

"Yes, sir?" I said.

"We want a couple cheeseburgers."

"Excellent choice. I like mine with lettuce and tomato, Heinz 57, and French fried potatoes."

"Huh?"

"That's from a Jimmy Buffett song."

"We don't want a song," screeched his girlfriend. "We want food!"

"We're hungry, too!" hollered the man with the dozen kids. Maybe to prove his point, one of his older sons picked a booger out of his nose and popped it into his mouth. The dad grabbed a laminated menu and basically ordered some of everything. "Gimme thirteen burgers, this smoked-fish dip, conch fritters, grouper nuggets, a chicken quesadilla, some hot wings, and a basket of fries and onion rings."

"Add in some pureed carrots for Charlene," said the mom. "She's a baby. She can't eat grouper nuggets, Joel."

The dad nodded. "I'll have some pureed carrots, too. Mix 'em into a vanilla milk shake."

Gloria and I nearly puked. Then we went to work.

It was a food fiasco.

Our only hope was to change everybody's order to something we could actually cook.

I went out front to address our hungry crowd, remembering Grandpa's advice about the power of a good story.

"You know, folks, I forgot to mention our Sunday special: Fantastically Famous Floridian Frankfurters Flambé!"

"What are those?" asked the tattooed guy.

"Handcrafted sausages that sizzle like the sand in the sun. Each juicy link is topped with sunny yellow mustard and sea-green pickle relish. The bun is as soft as an inflatable pool float. It's like eating a weeklong vacation on the Gulf of Mexico, only slightly less salty. Yes, our famous Florida dogs will definitely put your mouth in a sunshine state of mind! The one thing missing from your official Florida meal is orange juice, which is why we serve our hot dogs with an Orange Sproke."

"What's a Sproke?" asked the tattooed man.

"Only the most refreshing beverage ever created here at the Banana Shack!"

Everybody was in. We served two dozen hot dogs, several trays of microwaved fries, and sixteen cups of Orange Sproke. (That's Coke, Sprite, and Fanta Orange all mixed together.)

Our diners were happy.

We could relax. The lunch rush was over.

But then we got our first room service order.

The Right Side of the Menu

"Yeah, this is room 228," slobbered a voice on the other end of the line when I snatched up the phone behind the counter of the Banana Shack. "I'd like to place a room service order."

"Sure," I said. "No problem, sir."

I grabbed a pen and a ruled green pad.

"Okay, I'll have a couple burgers. Some oysters, with extra cocktail sauce."

I covered the mouthpiece and turned to Gloria. "Do we have oysters?"

She dragged a wooden bushel filled with gray shellfish out from under the sink.

"I think so. But they're totally raw," she reported.

"That's how you're supposed to eat them."

"Ewww. Gross."

"Yeah. Slimy, too." I went back to the phone. "Yes, sir. We have oysters."

"Are they fresh?" the guy asked.

"Um, they haven't been opened."

"Bring me two dozen. And one of those hot dogs everybody's eating. No, make that three. And some fries. Toss in onion rings, too."

I had to flip to the next page of the order pad.

Gloria threw everything together and loaded it onto a huge tray that I sort of balanced on my shoulder for the steep mountain climb up to the second floor.

The man in room 228, who looked like a body-builder who'd already bulked up, started grabbing oysters, shucking them open with a butter knife, and slurping them down before I even finished setting the tray on his kitchenette table.

"Charge it to my room," he said with his mouth full of raw shellfish. He bit into a hot dog. "Ugh. What's this stuff on top?"

"Tartar sauce," I said. "We ran out of pickle relish. And what's tartar sauce except pickle relish and mayonnaise?"

"It's disgusting is what it is." He chomped on an onion ring. "Okay. That's just cold, soggy, and repulsive. Now I need to wash *that* taste out of my mouth, too."

He peeled open the burger bun to reveal my

very well-done (okay, charred) meat patty. "Wow. Jimbo is way off his game today."

"Actually, sir, the Banana Shack is under new management."

"Really?" The guy sucked down a few more oysters. Since they were raw, my cooking couldn't hurt them.

"Yes, sir. And we'll be offering some brand-new menu selections. Do you like grilled cheese sandwiches?"

"What kind of cheese?"

"The orange kind in the plastic wrappers."

"I liked Jimbo's burgers better."

"We all did. . . ."

"Where'd he go?"

Instead of spinning a story, I decided to go with the honest answer.

"Um, jail."

"What? Why?"

"We think he might've been involved in the theft of the Twittleham Tiara and a guest's phone."

"Jimbo?" He pried open another oyster. "No way. Jimbo's a good guy. A righteous dude of the first degree, man." He gulped the slick boogery gunk out of the shell. "If he isn't here anymore, I might need to check out. . . ."

"But we couldn't let him stay. Not after we saw what he did."

"You saw him steal the tiara?"

"Not exactly. But we have a video of him breaking into the British butler's room."

We couldn't afford to lose any more guests, so I pulled out my phone and showed him the video clip I'd had Mr. Ortega forward to me.

"Wrong room," he said, still chewing a rubbery lump of oyster.

"Excuse me?"

"Wrong. Room."

The Whole Picture

"That was my food," said the man in 228, gulping down another slip 'n' slide oyster.

"Are you sure?"

"Of course I'm sure!" He wiped his mouth with the back of his hand. "Who forgets coconut shrimp, grouper nuggets, coconut-cashew-crusted mahimahi, sides of coleslaw and fries, with home-made key lime pie and cheesecake for dessert? Mmm-mmm. Memorable meal, man. On my top-ten list."

"But why did Jimbo bang on the butler's door?"

"Because I gave him the wrong room number."

I waited for him to crack open another oyster and glug it down.

"See, I'm in 228. The butler was in 227. I couldn't remember my number when I called down for room service, so I looked at my key fob, which I had accidentally dropped into my hot-fudge sundae the night before. I thought I'd licked it clean, but I hadn't. Anyway, the eight sort of looked like a seven. I heard all that banging on the veranda and went out to apologize to Jimbo for giving him the wrong room number. He brought the food into my room, set me up here at the table. You want to see the key lime pie? I saved the crust in the mini-fridge. . . ."

My stomach was starting to feel a little queasy.

"No thanks," I told him. "I'm good."

Fact: sometimes you need more than a quick video clip to see the whole picture. According to America's Biggest Eater, two seconds after Mr. Ortega blocked the camera lens, Jimbo quit banging on the butler's door and went into room 228.

The deputies had arrested the wrong guy.

And it was my fault.

I found Mom with a mountain of dirty linen in the laundry room and told her the news. She called the sheriff's office in Largo.

"We made a horrible mistake," she said to whoever was on the other end of the call. "Jimbo didn't do it. No. We don't know who did. We just know *he* didn't. Is he there? Can I talk to him? Thanks."

About a minute later, Jimbo must've picked up the phone in Largo.

"We're so sorry, Jimbo," said Mom. "We jumped to a very bad conclusion."

Jimbo accepted Mom's apology but said he needed to take "a little break" from work and that he might or might not come back.

"Indecision may or may not be my problem," he told her. (That's a line from a Jimmy Buffett song.)

"How are you and Gloria managing in the kitchen?" Mom asked after ending the call with Jimbo.

"Fine," I said, because she had a worried look on her face. Well, more worried than usual. "We're tweaking the menu, making it work."

"Great," Mom said with a sigh of relief. "I really appreciate it, P.T."

I headed back to the Banana Shack, where Gloria was examining the wooden bushel we'd found all those raw oysters in. There was a tag on it.

"Jimbo didn't do it," I told her.

I filled her in on what I'd learned up in 228. The whole time I was telling the tale (adding in some pretty gross slurp noises to help paint the scene, because details are what make a story sparkle), Gloria wasn't really paying attention. She kept staring at a tag dangling off the oyster basket.

"Interesting," she mumbled when I finished.

"So," I said, "we need a new suspect. I think we should talk to Lady Lilly again. Watching the video for the billionth time, I saw that flash of neon green racing out of the frame. Remember those bright green shorts Lilly was wearing? *Boom!* That was her!"

"Uh-huh," Gloria said absentmindedly.

"Oh-kay. Why, exactly, are you more interested in that tag than in solving this crime?"

"Because oysters are perishable, P.T. They're supposed to be kept refrigerated."

"So?"

"So we found ours under the sink. Near the garbage. Their expiration date was last week!"

Special Guests

We decided to permanently remove oysters from the menu.

It was mostly Gloria's idea.

"As your top business advisor," she said, "I suggest that going forward we stick to our knitting, do what we do best, and take the raw bar items off the Banana Shack menu before the Wonderland brand name becomes synonymous with vomit and/or diarrhea."

I checked my watch. It'd been about an hour since the guy in 228 had gobbled down his oyster gunk. If he was going to explode, it probably would've already happened. We'd dodged a bullet. Or something grosser.

"From now on," I vowed, "we only serve simple snacks and grilled cheese sandwiches." I snapped my fingers. "We should move the Morty D. Mouse statue over here. He's holding that cheese wedge. Maybe change the name of the restaurant to Chucky Cheezy."

Gloria shook her head. "Trademark issues, P.T. Trademark issues."

While we were brainstorming our special of the day (I suggested Cool Ranch Doritos; Gloria countered with Reese's Pieces), a sleek black sedan with tinted windows pulled into our parking lot. A man and woman in charcoal-gray business suits and sunglasses climbed out of the car and headed into the lobby.

"They look like spies," said Gloria.

Grandpa came out of his workshop, looking upset.

"They're from Disney!" he grumbled.

"What?" I said.

"Your mother called. Said I had to take over with the laundry because she had to talk to some very important visitors from Walt Disney World. Ha! You'd think she was in there with Mickey and Minnie. Sneaky little tourist-stealing rodents . . ."

Muttering under his breath, Grandpa headed off to the laundry room.

I flipped the sign hanging on one of the thatched-roofed restaurant's bamboo poles from "Open" to "Closed."

"Come on," I said to Gloria. "We need to see what this is all about."

We hurried into the lobby just as the two Disney suits were finishing up with Mom.

"In conclusion, Ms. Wilkie," said the lady, "we are very eager to keep on schedule with our new attraction inside Cinderella Castle."

"If your cook will simply return the tiara," said the man, "Lord and Lady Pettybone, as well as Walt Disney World, promise that no charges will be brought against him."

"We have so many young fans eager to see the exhibit," said the lady. "We'd really hate to disappoint them."

"I wouldn't!" said Grandpa.

His voice was sort of muffled because he was on the other side of the big glass windows, carrying a laundry basket filled with towels.

You people are so dopey you make me grumpy!

Mom rapped her knuckles on the glass, then flicked her wrist. Grandpa shuffled away.

"Look," Mom said, turning back to the two Disney executives, "we'd love nothing better than to give His Lordship and Her Ladyship back their tiara. But despite what you may have heard on the radio, our cook didn't steal it. Neither did our maid."

The Disney lady looked puzzled. "Then why was the cook recently arrested?"

I raised my hand.

"Mostly because of me."

Lady-in-Waiting

"**W**e really need to figure out who stole the tiara," I said to Gloria after the Disney people left and Mom went upstairs to clean more rooms.

"So who's at the top of our suspect list?" asked Gloria. "The disgruntled butler, Digby?"

I shook my head. "Lady Lilly. Digby told us how much she loves that tiara. Maybe she didn't want to let it go. Maybe that's why she was running out of frame in the video. Maybe we caught her trying to make her getaway!"

Gloria gave me an arched eyebrow. "Seriously?"

"Sure. What if she had the tiara tucked under her arm like a football and went running off to find a good place to hide it?"

Now both of Gloria's eyebrows went up. "P.T.,

if I may, you're usually more directionally accurate than that."

"Huh? What does that mean?"

"Your theory is idiotic. Lilly Pettybone jammed a priceless diamond-and-pearl-studded tiara under her arm as if it were a football and hid it someplace? Where? In a garbage can?"

"Look," I said, "we know Lilly lied to the butler at least once about locking the box. She's definitely hiding something, even if it isn't the Twittleham Tiara. We need to go talk to her again."

"Fine. But let's go around the back way. We might be able to avoid Mr. Conch and Veronica. They're always lurking in the lobby."

It was nearly three in the afternoon. The sun was beaming its way through the towering clouds. It was prime tanning and pool-dipping time. Gloria and I both figured Lilly would be regally lounging in her chair.

We were correct.

"Did you bring me more movie souvenirs?" Lilly asked eagerly.

"No," I said, pulling out my phone. "We want to show you a video."

"Brilliant. Is it *Beach Party Surf Monkey*?"

"No," I said. "The DVD hasn't dropped yet."

"Look for it this fall," added Gloria.

"This little movie stars somebody besides Pinky Nelligan and Cassie McGinty," I told Lilly. "It stars *you*!"

I showed her the video.

"That green blur," I said. "That's you. Those are your neon-green shorts."

"Quite right. I remember running past the servant carrying all that food."

"Where were you going in such a hurry?" asked Gloria.

"Down to the sand sculpture exhibition. The team behind your motel had just set off their spectacular fireworks display. I didn't want to miss it."

"And where did you put the tiara before you ran out the door?" I asked.

"I told you. It was safely locked in its box in the butler's room."

"Was it?" I said. "Or were you still practicing your princess poses with it when your parents and Mr. Digby went to the art museum?"

Lilly bristled. "Excuse me, but you are not permitted to speak to me that way. I am the heir to the Pettybone family title. Now, if you two could kindly move, I would appreciate it. You're blocking my sun."

My phone dinged in my hand.

I had an incoming text.

Pinky Nelligan was back in town.

I grinned.

We weren't done with Lady Lilly.

It was time to play the Pinky card!

Pinky Power

In case you forgot, Pinky Nelligan is our middle school bud who became an instant movie star sensation when he took over the lead role in *Beach Party Surf Monkey.*

How'd a kid from St. Pete Beach land a major role in a big-budget Hollywood movie? Well, first the original star, singing sensation Aidan Tyler (who couldn't act his way out of a paper bag), quit.

And then, like any good friend, I put in a word with the producers about my musically talented classmate Pinky.

So, yeah, he sort of owed me.

I texted Pinky back. Asked him to meet us at the Conch Reef Resort. He was poolside fifteen minutes later because he has a very speedy brand-new eighteen-gear Italian bicycle. You can buy that kind of stuff after you become a movie star.

"Oh, my gosh!" gasped Lady Lilly when Pinky strolled over to her chair. "You're you!"

"Yeah," said Pinky with the same wink he used in the movie. "I'm me."

I'd tipped him off about what was going on. Pinky had been trailed around the pool by about fifteen fans, but he acted like he only had eyes for Lilly.

Gloria and I drifted over to join Pinky and his gaggle of adoring fans.

"Yo!" said Pinky as we locked hands in a dudely handshake. "P.T.! My main man. And Gloria O. The brains behind the operation. What's shaking, you two?"

"Not much," I said. "Just trying to find out what happened with some missing jewelry at the Wonderland."

"To be specific," said Gloria, "the Twittleham Tiara."

Pinky leaned in and took Lilly's hand. "Wow. I totally dig jewelry. Everybody in Hollywood does. Do you know anything about this missing tiara, Lady Lilly?"

She looked dazed, like she'd fainted even though she was wide awake.

"Why, yes," she said. "I suppose I do. You see, Father and Mum wanted me to go to a dreary art museum with them. But I wanted to stay home and practice my proper princess posture."

Pinky nodded sympathetically. "Of course you did. Posture is very important. Especially in the movies. Nobody wants to see you slump on the big screen."

Lilly shivered and made a squiggly, dolphinish sound.

"Tell me more," said Pinky.

"Well, Digby, our butler, agreed to leave the Twittleham Tiara unlocked. I guess I whined a little to convince him. I might've even threatened to hold my breath until I turned blue."

"Hey," said Pinky, "no judgments."

"Pinky?"

"Yeah, Lilly?"

"You're even dreamier in person than you are in the movies."

"Right back at ya. Go on. What happened next?"

"I was having a grand time, pretending it was my coronation day! I paraded around Digby's room, perfectly balancing the tiara on my head. I waved out the windows to my imaginary peasants below as if I were on the balcony at Buckingham Palace."

"So how long did all this waving and prancing around take?" asked Gloria, who wasn't as into girly-girl stuff as Lilly.

"Goodness, I don't remember exactly. I was giving quite the rousing speech to Digby's mirror when I heard the fireworks exploding down on the beach. I raced to the window and saw that sand sculptor waving up at me, inviting me to come down and join in the celebration!"

"So, Lilly," said Pinky, reaching out to take both her hands in his. "You saw the fireworks."

"That's right."

"You dashed out of the room."

"Yes."

"Were you still wearing the tiara?"

"Of course not."

"Cool. So one final question: What did you do with it?"

49

Couch Potato Crown

"**I** suppose I tossed it on the sofa," said Lilly.

"You tossed it on the sofa?" I couldn't believe it.

"Well, I couldn't very well wear it down to the beach, could I?"

"Of course you couldn't," said Pinky, playing the smiling good cop to my scowling bad cop.

"So you just chucked it on the couch?" I said.

"The couch in Digby's sitting room had nice, plump cushions," said Lilly. "It was a very soft landing."

"Did you close the door when you left?" asked Gloria.

Lilly's nose twitched a little. "Maybe."

"Maybe?" said Pinky.

"Oh, Pinky. I was in a rush to join in the celebration on the beach."

"Of course you were."

"All I remember is dashing out the door. But I'm sure I closed it behind me. Otherwise the servant with the heavy food tray should've said something as I ran past him. It's a servant's duty to take care of any irregularities, such as open doors."

"He's not a servant," said Gloria. "Jimbo's a chef."

"A chef I need to apologize to," I said.

"Whatever for?" asked Lilly. It sounded like she'd never apologized for anything in her life.

Pinky let go of Lilly's hands. He turned to me and Gloria. "You guys got everything you need?"

"No," said Gloria. "Were the curtains still open when you left the butler's room?"

"I suppose," said Lady Lilly. "It was Digby's room. If he wanted the curtains closed, he should've closed them himself."

"So anybody strolling past the window to room 227 could've seen the sparkling tiara sitting there on the couch?"

"Only if they were nosey parkers, snooping into someone else's private room—which, by the way, is extremely bad form."

"Riiiight," said Gloria. "Bad form."

Pinky checked his phone.

"It's my agent," he said (even though from where I was standing I could see that the only thing on his phone was his Surf Monkey screen saver).

"Emergency audition. I need to run. Good-bye, Lady Lilly."

He kissed her on the cheek.

After he did that, *I* totally owed *him*.

• • •

"So now our pool of suspects includes everybody who might've strolled by Digby's window," said Gloria as we made our way through the Sandapalooza crowds on the beach.

(By the way, the Jabba the Hutt sculpture sponsored by the Bikini Hut was incredible.)

"Everybody with a master key is still on the list, too," I added. "Except Clara."

"Net-net," said Gloria, "considering the keys and the open curtains, we're talking just about everybody at the Wonderland."

"Except Clara," I said. "And Jimbo. Other than that, we're nowhere."

"With nothing," added Gloria.

To make matters worse, we'd reached the Conch Reef Resort's sand sculpture, that all-you-can-eat buffet made out of sand. Veronica was there. With a bullhorn.

"Vote for Conch for best in show!" she screamed as she handed out coupons. She was dressed up like a strip of bacon. "And tomorrow, before you start bakin' in the sun, get a sizzling ten percent off our world-class bacon-rific breakfast buffet!"

"She's stealing our thunder," I muttered.

"She's also stealing our customers," said Gloria. "While we've been focused on the tiara, our competition has been free to growth hack their way onto our turf."

"Fine," I said. "Game on. It's time for a food fight!"

Chunky Funky Monkey
to the Rescue

Like I said, sometimes I watch cooking shows on cable TV.

I remembered an episode with a recipe for the perfect sandwich to feature at the Banana Shack to win back some customers. I did a quick Google search and found it. It was simple and totally safe. There were no oysters anywhere in the recipe.

Gloria and I turned on all the light strings around the café and went to work.

"We need bread," I said, twisting the knob to ignite the griddle heat.

"Check," said Gloria from the pantry.

"And all the stuff for s'mores—minus the graham crackers. Marshmallows, chocolate . . ."

"Check and check."

"How about cream cheese?"

"Got it."

"Butter?"

"A huge industrial-sized block of it."

"Bananas?"

"Two bunches left over from breakfast."

"Chunky peanut butter?"

Gloria stuck her head out the pantry door. "Isn't that going a bit too far?"

"Nope. Like Grandpa always says, when you're out to dazzle, too much is never enough!"

But just having a fantastic sandwich wouldn't put us over the top. The sandwich was the steak. (Well, not really, because there wasn't any beef in a Chunky Funky Monkey, just cream cheese, marshmallows, sliced bananas, chocolate chunks, and a smear of chunky peanut butter, but, hey, sometimes you need to use a metaphor or two when you're telling a story.) It was time to add the sizzle.

First we cooked up a dozen Chunky Funky Monkeys. Talk about your gooey deliciousness.

GRILLED AND GOOEY AWESOMENESS!

Grandpa smelled the first batch cooking from his workshop and came over to lend a hand.

"This is like old times, P.T. You know, I worked as a short-order cook when I was in high school. The waitress would holler, 'Burn one, black and blue, drag it through the garden, and let it walk,' and I knew exactly what to do."

"Run away? Find a new job?"

"Nope, nope, nope. In dinerspeak, that means a well-done cheeseburger with lettuce, tomato, and onion—to go!"

Grandpa took over flipping the sandwiches on the grill.

Gloria ran up to the lobby and raided our souvenir stock so she could bring me a sock-monkey puppet.

Next we slipped the *Beach Party Surf Monkey* original cast CD into Jimbo's boom box and rigged up our own karaoke microphone.

It was showtime!

Monkey Business

I ducked down behind the counter with the puppet on my hand.

Gloria hit the play button on the CD player. I made the puppet dance to the show tunes.

We attracted a small crowd, so I bantered with kids lining up to order sandwiches.

I made the Surf Monkey sock puppet say all sorts of goofy stuff. Kids were laughing. Parents were smiling. The Banana Shack cash register was ringing.

It was just like the good old days.

You know—last week.

Grandpa and Gloria kept serving up the sandwiches, and before long, the café was packed—with happy motel guests and hungry folks from the Sandapalooza down on the beach.

We sold out in under an hour.

"Great show, P.T.," said Grandpa. "Better than anything at Disney World. Especially now that they don't have that Twittleham Tiara to brag about."

"We need to go to the grocery store," suggested Gloria. "Restock our key ingredients. The Chunky Funky Monkey sandwich and show could be the silver bullet we need to scramble back to the top of the hospitality heap on St. Pete Beach."

"Woo-hoo!" I shouted. "Sprokes for everybody!"

Our celebration was cut short by the hungry muscleman in room 228. The guy who'd slurped down all those raw oysters.

He came out of his room, looking green around the gills and clutching his stomach.

"I'm not feeling so good," he said, teetering behind the balcony railing. "Don't eat any of that kid's food. It might make you—"

He didn't get to finish that thought.

Because he was too busy hurling over the railing.

And of course some of what spewed out ended up floating in the pool.

Yep.

All those slimy oysters were back in the water.

The Darkest Night

Sunday night, things didn't look any brighter.

And not just because clouds were blocking the moon.

Some of our new "freebie" guests decided to use our Freddy the Frog slide as a drying rack for their kids' diapers, which they'd rinsed out in the pool.

A bunch of the rowdy college kids who'd swooped in after Mom advertised our bargain rates kept trying to tip over our giant Ponce de León Muffler Man statue.

I had to threaten to call the cops.

They left the Muffler Man alone and attacked Dino the Dinosaur until they realized they couldn't cow tip a four-legged fiberglass beast with its feet anchored in concrete.

Gloria and I were sitting near the pool (which I

had to skim clean with a net after the oyster explosion incident), watching a bunch of college kids sliding down Freddy the Frog. They snagged a few diapers along the way.

"The Wonderland is turning into the opposite of Walt Disney World," I told Gloria. "They're the happiest place on earth; we're the saddest."

"Technically," said Gloria, who's a stickler for stuff like this, "'the Happiest Place on Earth' is the official tagline for Disneyland in California. I believe the Magic Kingdom in Orlando is 'the Most Magical Place on Earth.'"

"Well, we're the most miserable."

Gloria sighed. "And we were doing so well."

"Yeah. We *were*. Past tense."

"But then," said Gloria, sounding a little like her dad when he wraps up a story on TV, "somebody stole the Twittleham Tiara and, with it, the Wonderland's bright and shiny future."

A thought I'd been trying to get rid of bubbled up in my brain and, before I could stop it, tumbled out of my mouth.

"Do you think Grandpa could've done it?"

"What?" said Gloria.

"He doesn't like Disney. Actually, he kind of *hates* Disney on account of October 1, 1971."

"True, but—"

"I'm not saying he stole the tiara. If he did,

I'm sure he would've turned it in the second Lord Snootypants accused Clara. But he sure seems happy that Disney doesn't have it. Maybe *too* happy."

Gloria stood up. "It's late, P.T. Dad needs me to watch his broadcast tonight. He's going to try out a new catchphrase. If you want to investigate your grandfather, you're going to have to do that on your own."

She walked around the pool and started climbing the staircase up to the second floor. When she reached the third step, she turned around, looked at me, and shook her head.

Yep. I couldn't believe what a jerk I was being, either.

Suspecting Grandpa?

But still, he really, really, *really* didn't like Disney World.

I decided I had to be sure.

I had to go search Grandpa's workshop.

Going from Bad to Workshop

It was nearly eleven o'clock at night.

I tiptoed around to the front of the motel and saw the familiar glow of Mom's TV on the other side of the curtains of room 101. I also saw two familiar silhouettes: Mom's and Grandpa's.

Most nights, they got together in Mom's room to talk over the day and watch the eleven o'clock news on channel ten, WTSP, because that's where Mr. Ortega manned the late-night sports desk.

Sports wouldn't come on for fifteen, twenty minutes.

That meant I had plenty of time to sneak into Grandpa's workshop and see if he had a priceless diamond tiara stashed anywhere.

Grandpa lives in a one-bedroom apartment over what sort of resembles a wooden garage near the swimming pool. I was pretty sure that if he'd stolen the Twittleham Tiara, he would've squirreled it away in his cramped workshop. The place was cluttered with all sorts of goofy gewgaws, making for some great hiding places.

Grandpa was currently working on a bunch of fiberglass statues for the Banana Shack—stuff he'd purchased at restaurant liquidation sales: a pudgy chef holding a menu board, one of those burgerloving Big Boys in the red-checked coveralls, and a lip-smacking hot dog squirting ketchup on top of its head.

"Where would he hide the tiara?" I wondered aloud.

I opened up a bunch of big coffee cans. They were mostly filled with nuts and bolts and springs and stuff. I checked out some cardboard boxes. Nothing resembling the jeweled tiara was stuffed inside. I flicked on a gooseneck lamp and swung it around like a searchlight.

Something sparkled on a far shelf. Whatever it was, it was extremely bedazzling.

The tiara?

I rushed over to examine it.

It was an old pickle jar filled with sequins and spangles and shiny baubles. The kind of junk Grandpa hot-glued onto statues to make them shimmer in the sun.

The overhead lights flickered on.

"P.T.?"

It was Grandpa.

"Hey, Grandpa."

"What're you doing back here?"

"Nothing."

"Really? Because it looked like you were searching for something."

"Found it," I said, rattling the jar full of sparkly stuff. "Sure is shiny. Just like that Twittleham Tiara."

Grandpa's head drooped. His shoulders sagged.

"Is that what you were back here looking for? The tiara? You think *I* stole it?"

"No. Of course not."

"Don't lie, P.T. If I've taught you anything, it's that there's a big difference between telling a story and telling a lie."

"I know, but—"

"A story tries to lead you to the truth. A lie only helps you hide from it."

I swallowed hard. I couldn't lie to Grandpa. I had to tell him the truth.

"Okay," I said. "Did you, by any chance, steal the tiara out of the Cassie McGinty Suite?"

"And why would I do that?"

"To get back at Disney World for what they did to you all those years ago."

"Is that what you think, P.T.?"

I'd never seen him look so sad.

"I'm sorry, Grandpa."

"Me too, Phineas. Me too."

He climbed up the creaky wooden steps to his sleeping loft.

I watched him disappear into the darkness. The closest thing I'd ever had to a father was turning his back on me.

I couldn't blame him.

I would've turned my back on me, too.

Evil Sand Creatures

Feeling worse than I had in a long, long time, I headed down to the beach.

Sometimes the sound of the pounding surf can make me feel better. Mostly because the waves keep coming, no matter what. They never give up. The ocean never quits.

But it was kind of creepy to be walking through a shadowy world of giant dragons and castles, pirates and superheroes, dolphins and mermaids—all of them made out of sand.

I saw Travis and Darryl sitting around a small driftwood fire in front of their Surf Monkey creation. Fact: I definitely needed to have a father-son chat with the guy I had a hunch might be my dad. (I'd just been too busy with the never-ending string of motel disasters to confirm it with Mom.)

"Hey, guys," I said.

"Well, hey there, son," said Travis. "What're you doing down here so late?"

"Isn't it past your bedtime?" joked Darryl.

"I, uh, couldn't sleep," I told them.

"Bummer," said Darryl. "We're sleeping down here tonight."

"Seriously?"

"Yeah," said Travis. "Camping out on the beach. Nothin' like it. Salt air. Twinkly stars." He patted the sand. "Take a seat, little man. Admire our crowning achievement while you can. It won't be here after tomorrow—and neither will we."

"Do you have to leave?" I asked.

Travis laughed. "Son, the whole sand sculpture shebang is shutting down tomorrow afternoon. They'll announce the winners at five. We'll pack and skedaddle before five-thirty. Heck, we'll be in Georgia before the bulldozers show up to plow everything down."

"But don't you want to stick around?" I asked. "We've been so busy up at the motel we've hardly spent any time together. Plus you and my mom haven't had a chance to talk."

"Talk? About what?"

"You know. The old days. Over in Orlando. Right before you left Florida. Right before I was born?"

"There he goes!" said Darryl. "Winner, winner, chicken dinner. Mr. Conch was right."

Travis laughed. "He sure was."

I was confused. "Right about what?"

"Kid," said Travis, "I ain't your daddy."

"When Mr. Conch signed us up for this gig," said Darryl, "he told us how your daddy left town before you were even born."

"Why was Mr. Conch talking to you guys about my father?" I asked.

Travis just shrugged.

"I reckon he has his reasons," said Darryl. "But I gotta tell you, kid, I'm a little hurt you went with Travis instead of me."

"Well," said Travis, "sorry to burst your bubble, son, but I am not now nor have I ever been your father. It's an impossibility."

"What do you mean?" I asked foolishly.

"Come on, kid. I saw your mother this afternoon when I breezed past the lobby. She's not exactly my type."

Hearing Travis talk that way about Mom, I was glad he wasn't my father.

I also wanted to punch him in the nose.

But I didn't.

I hadn't thought my night could get any worse.

I'd been wrong.

I Can't Sand It!

Monday morning came pretty quickly because I was still awake at one, two, and three a.m.

I lay in my bed, marveling at how stupid I'd been. About Travis. About Jimbo. About Grandpa. About shellfish.

When I finally fell asleep, I had a horrible dream. Travis and Darryl turned the Wonderland into a life-size *sand* motel. One of those waves I used to like to hear pounding against the shore washed everything—our statues, our friends, our family— out into the Gulf.

When I woke up, I headed to the Banana Shack, figuring I'd try to cook breakfast for anybody who wanted a Chunky Funky Monkey first thing in the morning.

Wow. I hope our motel has nightmare insurance.

To my surprise, Gloria and Mr. Ortega were already behind the counter.

"I'm making pancakes," announced Mr. Ortega.

"With scrapple," said Gloria. "I found it in the fridge."

"Care to join us?" asked her dad.

I shrugged. "Sure. I guess."

"And might I make a suggestion?" said Mr. Ortega. "When everything's cooked up and ready to go, you should take a tray to that beautiful lady you call your mother. After all she's been through, she deserves breakfast in bed."

"Good idea."

"So hey, hey, Tampa Bay—it's time to get to it!"

"That's Dad's new catchphrase," explained Gloria. "He tried it out last night."

"I like it."

"Thanks, P.T." Mr. Ortega ladled batter onto the grill and dotted the bubbling mix with blueberries. "Any new leads on your investigation?"

"Not really," I said.

Gloria slapped a few slabs of scrapple onto the griddle. It sputtered and popped.

"Sorry my video clip couldn't seal the deal for you two," said Mr. O. "But don't warm up the team bus just yet. This thing isn't over. You just have a tough road to hoe."

"Um, Dad?" said Gloria. "I think you mean a 'tough row,' not a 'tough road.'"

"No, 'road' is what the big dogs say on ESPN."

"How do you hoe a road?"

Mr. Ortega flipped a pancake. "With a backhoe?"

Finally, something made me smile.

The first plate of breakfast food went on a tray with a glass of freshly squeezed orange juice that Mr. Ortega poured out of a jug he'd bought at a convenience store.

"Hang on," he said. "We need the finishing touch."

He plucked a pair of pink flowers off a nearby

shrub and tucked them into a tiny cut-glass vase he found under the counter.

"Perfect! Now go make your first room service delivery of the day, Mr. Wilkie. And when you two finish your breakfasts, it's time to turn up the heat. You need to go back out there and solve the case of the missing tiara."

"But we don't have any leads," I told him as I picked up the tray.

"Then find some."

"Fantastic idea, Dad," said Gloria, rolling her eyes. "I wonder why we didn't think of that."

"Hey, if the guy from 228 could clear Jimbo," he said, "maybe the folks in some of the other rooms could help you out, too."

I stood there. Dumbfounded.

Mr. Ortega was absolutely right.

"There might've been other witnesses!" I said.

He shot me a finger pistol. "Hey, hey, Tampa Bay—it's time to get to it!"

Knocking on Doors

Right after our pancake breakfast (which, by the way, was delicious and which Mom loved), Gloria and I headed upstairs to the second floor.

We took a platter of scrapple samples with us.

First we went to room 231.

A bunch of college kids, maybe six, were sharing the room.

"Um, hi, I'm from the Banana Shack," I announced when one of the sleepy-headed guys opened the door. "Were you here on Friday?"

"No," the guy said with a yawn. "We checked in yesterday, after a buddy tweeted us about the free-night deal."

That meant they couldn't've seen anything the day the tiara disappeared, because they hadn't been there.

"Well," I said, "as part of our new promotion,

you're entitled to a free scrapple sample during your stay. Would you like yours now?"

"No. What I'd like is to go back to sleep. Do you know what time it is?"

"Yes, sir. We're a full-service motel." I looked at my watch. "The time is now—"

He shut the door in my face.

We had given room 230 to Travis and Darryl, because they were our sand-sculpting team (and they were still sleeping on the beach).

"We could try the rooms on the other side of the staircase, too," said Gloria. "They might've seen something."

"Definitely. But we still have three more on this side."

"One more. I'm in 233. Dad's in 234."

"Which leaves us 232."

I rapped my knuckles lightly on the door.

"Yes?" said a sweet and sunny voice on the other side. "Who is it?"

"Room service."

"That's very nice. But I didn't order anything."

"We're giving away free samples of scrapple."

Someone pulled back the curtain in the window near the door. It was Helen Nelson, the lady from Canada who always booked the same four-week vacation with us every year.

I waved at her.

She smiled and waved at me.

I waved back.

She waved back, too.

It could've gone on all day. Canadian people are very, very polite.

"We brought you scrapple!" I announced.

"Really?" said Ms. Nelson. "I'd love to play!"

She opened the door.

"Where's the game board?" she asked when she saw that all I had was a plate of rectangular meat blocks.

I explained to her what scrapple was.

She didn't want any.

Because, like I said, I explained to her what scrapple was.

"Can I ask you a couple questions?"

"Why certainly, Phineas."

"Did you see anything suspicious out here on the balcony Friday?"

"You mean before those college kids moved into 229? Because I think one of those boys is sleeping on an inflatable hippopotamus pool float, and that's *very* suspicious if you ask me."

"Before that," said Gloria. "Did you see anything out of the ordinary?"

"Just those Roman candles they shot off down at the Surf Monkey sand sculpture. I believe fireworks are forbidden on the beach. . . ."

I nodded. "Our sand sculptors are from out of town. They don't know all the rules."

"Well, I'll be sure to tell them. Especially that Travis. He sure is a cutie-patootie, eh?"

"Yes, ma'am. Did you see anything else, Ms. Nelson?"

"No. But since you're here, Phineas . . ."

"Yes, ma'am?"

"I was wondering: could I change rooms, like that handsome young Travis and his friend did?"

"Excuse me?"

"They're in 230 now, correct?"

"That's right."

"Well, Friday afternoon, not too long after his buddy set off the illegal fireworks down on the beach, I saw Travis coming out of room 227 with his bright blue sand bucket. If they're happy with 230, I'd love to take over 227. It's so much closer to the steps."

"You saw Travis coming out of 227?" I said. "On Friday?"

"That's right."

I stood up on tiptoes and kissed Ms. Nelson on the cheek.

"Thank you!"

"For what?"

"Everything!"

Sandtastic News!

Gloria and I raced to my room to retrieve the sand sample we'd swept into the plastic ice-bucket liner when we'd examined the butler's room.

"This sand probably fell out of Travis's bucket," I said.

"While he was frantically scooping out a shallow hole to bury the Twittleham Tiara!" added Gloria.

She was right. A sand bucket would have made a fantastic portable hiding place for the jeweled tiara. Travis could have covered it up and waltzed back to his room without anyone asking any questions.

"But how do we link the sand we found in the room to Travis?" I puzzled out loud.

"If it's heavy sand," said Gloria, "that'll tie it to one of the sand sculptures."

I nodded, remembering that Travis and Darryl

had told us the sculptors used a different kind of sand from what we'd find on the beach. It had a different texture and was thicker.

All the other sculptors were using what Travis had called "cheaper, inferior material." Because the Michelsandgelo team had insisted on "first-class" sand, it'd be super easy to tie them to the sand we found in the butler's room.

"If the sand in this bag matches the sand in the Surf Monkey sculpture, then we've got 'em!" I told Gloria. "No one else is using that type of sand."

"True," said Gloria. "But how do we get the tiara back?"

"One step at a time," I said. "First we need to see if the sand matches."

"And how are we going to do that?"

I snapped my fingers. "Ms. Carey!"

"Our science teacher?"

"We can put both sand samples under a microscope, like they do on the CSI shows with hairs and fibers. Make the match."

"Today's a holiday, P.T. The contest ends this afternoon. Travis and Darryl and all the other sand sculptors will be gone by the time we're back in science class."

"So we have to work fast."

"School's closed," said Gloria. "That's why we aren't there."

"Good thing science never takes a holiday," I said, reminding Gloria of Ms. Carey's speech to us on Friday.

"Okay," said Gloria, her confidence clearly building. "This might work. Maybe."

She took a long, thoughtful pause.

"But what?" I asked.

"Well, not to be a buzzkill, but who's going to extract a sand sample from the Surf Monkey sculpture without Travis and Darryl getting suspicious? If they figure out we're onto them, they may bolt."

"And take the tiara with them."

"Exactly. I'm sorry, P.T., but we may need to go back and sharpen our pencils, rethink this. Maybe we should call the police."

"Um, I don't think we should do that."

"Why not?"

"Because they basically told Mom not to call them anymore after we made the mistake with Jimbo."

"But if we have proof . . ."

"We don't. All we have right now is a plastic bag with a tablespoon of sand in it."

"So what are our next steps?"

I snapped my fingers. Again.

"Chunky Funky Monkey delivery!"

"Huh?"

"We take Travis and Darryl an early lunch."

"Oh-kay. But how, exactly, does taking them sandwiches get us our sand?"

"Easy," I told her. "I can be extremely clumsy when I put my mind to it. I have a feeling I might drop the tray—right on Surf Monkey and Poseidon!"

Sand Which We Want

We hit the Banana Shack and loaded up a tray with two sandwiches, a couple of bags of chips, soda cans, and empty paper cups.

Those paper cups were the most important part of the meal.

"Hi, guys," I said merrily when we arrived at the Surf Monkey sand sculpture. "Who's hungry for lunch?"

"Lunch?" said Darryl. "It's only ten o'clock. Nobody eats lunch before noon."

I raised the tray to show Travis the gooey sandwiches.

His nose started twitching. Darryl's, too.

It's hard to resist the alluring scent of chocolate, banana, peanut butter, and cream cheese all melted together in grilled deliciousness.

Darryl reached for a sandwich.

I raised the tray an inch or two, tilting it at a thirty-degree angle. My geometry teacher would've been proud.

The plates and chip bags and soda cans and waxy cups slid downhill and tumbled off the edge of the tray.

"Whoops!"

I fake flinched and dumped the whole load.

"My bad."

"Let me help you clean up that mess," said Gloria.

We dropped to our knees and pretended to clean up.

What we were really doing was scooping up heavy-sand samples in that pair of paper cups.

While we were down on our knees, I couldn't help noticing that both Travis and Darryl were wearing leather tool belts full of sharp, pointy objects they could've used to pick the lock on room 227—if Lady Lilly hadn't just left the door wide open for them when she went running down to the beach to catch the fireworks display.

Wait a second, I thought. *Were the Roman candles a coincidence?*

Maybe Travis had seen Lady Lilly parading around in the room, wearing the tiara. With all those sparkling diamonds, it sure seemed like it would catch your eye, even all the way down on the beach.

Especially if you had binoculars to spy on the cook and guests up at the motel, like Travis did.

I figured he went upstairs and waited for Darryl to light the fireworks, hoping they would lure Lilly out of the room, which, of course, they did!

"So, um, do you guys still want the, uh, sandy sandwiches?" I asked when we had everything back on the tray.

"No thanks," said Travis. "But we'll take those two sodas."

"Sure." I tossed him both cans.

By the way, they were hot.

So I was pretty sure that with the added shaking from the tumble and toss, they'd explode the instant Travis and Darryl popped them open.

Fact: you say mean stuff about my mother, sooner or later you're gonna get an exploding geyser of hot, sticky soda—right in your face.

Science Project

"**Y**ou two are officially my favorite science students of all time!" gushed Ms. Carey as she led us down the middle school's deserted hallways to the science lab. "No one has ever asked to borrow a microscope on a school holiday."

"Well, it's kind of a CSI game we're playing," I said.

"Oh, I love those crime scene investigator shows. Las Vegas, Miami, New York. I watch 'em all. Love the science."

"Us too," I said.

"So what are we working with?" asked Ms. Carey. "Carpet fibers? Grass clippings?"

"Sand."

"Oh. CSI: Beach Patrol!"

"Exactly."

"We need to do a side-by-side comparison of two sand samples under the microscope," said Gloria.

We set up two microscopes and took turns eye-balling the evidence.

(By the way, sand looks unbelievably awesome under a microscope! You should try it.)

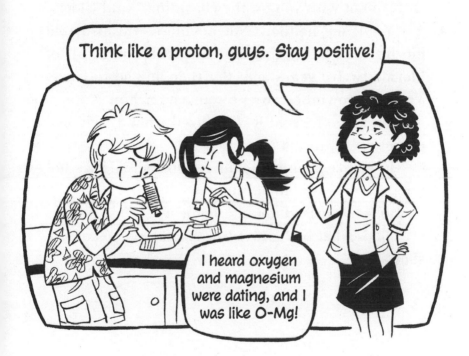

They were exactly the same. The sand from the butler's room matched the sand from the Surf Monkey sculpture! We'd connected the sand sculptors to the scene of the crime.

We thanked Ms. Carey and headed back to the Wonderland on our bikes.

"We need more evidence," said Gloria. "What do we know about the two sand sculptors? Anything?"

"I hung out with Travis a little," I admitted.

"What did you learn?"

"That he's very handsome and very charming and can spin a good story."

"I'm not with you on the charming," said Gloria.

"Yeah, me neither. Not anymore. He also told me he used to be the top sand sculptor in all of Florida twelve years ago. But then he had to leave. The heat down here was too much for him."

The instant I said it, I realized what Travis had meant.

He hadn't been complaining about Florida's hot temperatures and high humidity.

He was worried about "the heat."

That's what bad guys always call the cops on TV shows!

Sand Devils

Gloria and I hit the computer in the business center, which is really just the coffee room where we set out pastries for breakfast.

Nobody—except, of course, Gloria Ortega—has ever come to the Wonderland hoping to do business. But we do have a computer and a printer. Sometimes the printer even has paper in it. Sometimes.

After some random Googling, we dug up a string of articles from twelve years ago about "mysterious disappearances" and "unexplained thefts" taking place in hotels and motels near sand sculpture festival sites in Florida. Wallets, credit cards, jewelry, and expensive electronic gear were all reported missing.

One article we found, from a newspaper in Fort Myers, Florida, said:

Several guests at the hotel where the thefts took place reported seeing a man wearing cargo shorts, a tool belt, and a floppy sun hat "lurking" near rooms where the burglaries occurred. The man was later identified as Travis Shelton, a master sculptor who bills himself as "the Great Sandini." Shelton was a contestant in the American Sand Sculpting Championships taking place over the weekend on Fort Myers Beach. The sheriff's office found no evidence to implicate Shelton in the thefts, and reports that the investigation into the matter is ongoing.

"No wonder Travis quit competing in Florida," I said after reading the article. "The heat was definitely on."

"So why, after twelve years, did he decide to come back?" asked Gloria.

"I dunno. Maybe because Mr. Conch invited him. Maybe Travis and Darryl don't charge as much as other master sculptors. Maybe they're cheap, like that sand Mr. Conch wanted everybody to use."

"And maybe," said Gloria, "Travis and Darryl can afford to be cheap because they make their real money stealing stuff out of rooms. An interesting business model."

We did some more Googling to see if there had

been any reported thefts in hotels and motels near sand sculpture competitions in the Carolinas and California, the places where Travis had said he'd been competing over the past decade.

There had been.

"We need to search room 230. And we need to search it soon, because those guys are going to pull out of here at five-thirty—right after the closing ceremonies."

"Slight problem," said Gloria.

"What?"

"We can't search their rooms *before* they check out—not without a search warrant."

"We can if they let us."

"Huh?"

"If Darryl and Travis give us permission, we can poke around their room all we want."

"And how, exactly, is that going to happen?"

"I have an idea."

"Is it a good one?"

"Definitely. But we're going to need help."

"From who?"

The pieces of the puzzle were still sliding into place in my head. But a pretty solid plan was starting to take shape.

"Pinky," I said.

"No problem," said Gloria.

"We also need the fanciest video camera your dad has up in his room."

"How about a refurbished Sony PMW-300K1 XDCAM HD camcorder? He uses it sometimes to grab footage at games and practices."

"Works for me." I took a deep breath. "We also need Grandpa."

"Easy-peasy," said Gloria.

"Maybe not today."

"Why?"

"I kind of broke his heart last night."

Ketching Up with Grandpa?

I didn't know what to expect when Gloria and I got to Grandpa's workshop.

"Go ahead," said Gloria. "Knock on the door."

"He might be sleeping."

"No, P.T. He wakes up at six every morning."

"But what if—"

"Just knock!"

I did.

"Who is it?"

"Me," I said.

"And me," said Gloria.

"Oh. Me-me. Come in, come in. No. Wait. Hang on. First I have to hide this priceless diamond tiara my grandson thinks I stole from those Twittleham twits."

I pushed open the door.

"Hey, Grandpa," I said.

"Hello, Phineas." He was standing in front of the giant hot dog statue. "You ever wonder why a hot dog would squirt ketchup on his head?"

"I think it's his shampoo."

"For what? A hot dog is bald. It doesn't have hair. Maybe ketchup is like sunscreen in Hot Dog Land. Or cologne. Maybe all the hot dog ladies dig a hot dog dude who smells like tomatoes mixed with corn syrup."

Gloria chuckled. Me too.

"Grandpa?" I said.

"Yes, P.T.?"

"I'm sorry."

"Care to be more specific?"

"Yes. I am totally sorry for even thinking you could have had anything to do with stealing the Twittleham Tiara."

"And why is that?"

That stopped me in my tracks. I had to think for a second.

And then it hit me—the real reason Grandpa would never, ever steal anything out of any room in our motel.

He knew that Clara, or one of the other housekeepers, would be blamed for it.

"You would never do it," I said, "because Clara and Debbie and Edith and all the housekeepers are

·232·

like family. And we Wilkies never do anything to hurt our family."

Grandpa threw open his arms wide.

"Let all the people shout 'hallelujah'! My grandson is back!"

Gloria and I quickly brought Grandpa up to speed.

"So you think Travis and Darryl did it," said Grandpa, "not the butler?"

"Exactly," I said. "If we can get into their room and search it while they're not there, I'm pretty sure we'll find the tiara. There aren't that many places you can hide stuff in a motel room."

"True," said Grandpa. "But we can't just barge into a guest's room. That's against the law *and* the hospitality industry's code of ethics."

"But," I said, "what if the guests invited us to go into their room?"

"Go on. I'm listening."

"We pretend we're filming a documentary. Pinky Nelligan, the star of *Beach Party Surf Monkey,* is the host."

"Oh," said Grandpa, fishing a can of Cel-Ray soda out of his portable ice chest, "he's good. I'd watch Pinky read the phone book. Do they still make phone books?"

"Doesn't matter," I said. "Pinky's making a movie about the life of sand sculptors. We could call it *Sand Hoppers.*"

"Um, isn't that a type of flea?" asked Gloria.

"Not in this movie. Sand hoppers are artists who hop around from beach to beach, creating beautiful sculptures. Pinky and his camera crew are capturing their life on the road. Including a backstage, behind-the-scenes look at their living quarters!"

"I love it!" said Grandpa.

"So we need you to be our mature adult."

"P.T., this is me we're talking about here."

"It'll make the movie look more legit."

"Will you do it, Mr. Wilkie?" asked Gloria.

Grandpa shook his head. "Nope, nope, nope."

"Huh?" I said.

"I'm not your guy, P.T."

Wow.

I figured he was still mad at me.

Hey, Hey, Tampa Bay

"**W**e need Manny!" said Grandpa. "Gloria's father!"

"We were going to use his camera," said Gloria.

"Good. Use him, too. He'll know how to talk digital and pixels and all that technical stuff."

"You think he'll do it?" I asked Gloria.

"Definitely," she said. "He has the day off. Plus, he'll do anything to help you guys."

"Fantastic!" said Grandpa, eagerly rubbing his hands together. "I love it when a plan comes together. Hannibal used to say that on *The A-Team*."

Gloria and I just stared at him.

"*The A-Team*. It was a hit TV show."

We kept staring.

Grandpa flapped his hand at us. "Ah, never mind. But that George Peppard? One heck of an actor!"

"Riiiight," said Gloria. "I'll go grab Dad!"

"Hey," Grandpa said to me, "speaking of fantastic actors, shouldn't you hurry up and call Pinky to the set already?"

"On it!" I said, pulling out my phone.

Pinky was happy to help out. "Do I have to, you know, kiss Lady Lilly on the cheek again?"

"No," I promised him. Then I filled him in on our plan.

"Cool. You know, I've always wanted to fake-host a fake documentary."

"Meet us out back at the Banana Shack!"

"On my way."

Ten minutes later, our whole A-Team (that's what Grandpa insisted we call ourselves) assembled at the outdoor café. Mr. Ortega had a camcorder propped on his shoulder.

"Gloria filled me in on what's going down," he said. "Hey, hey, Tampa Bay. Let's get to it. It's time to put the biscuit in the bucket!"

"Um, yeah," said Pinky. "What Mr. Ortega just said."

"Thanks again, everybody," I said. "Here, Pinky. Gloria and I wrote up a script for you. You're playing you, but as a reporter doing a human-interest feature story."

"Cool. If they're humans, I'm interested."

"The whole idea is to get Travis and Darryl to

invite us to film inside their room. Because that's where we think they hid the stolen you-know-what."

"Towels?" said Pinky. "Did they steal a bunch of those fluffy pink beach towels you're only supposed to use at the pool? Because I love those things, man."

"We didn't concoct this elaborate caper to find a few missing towels, Pinky," said Gloria.

"Well, I would. Especially when they're warm, right out of the dryer."

"You guys?" I said. "The clock is ticking. We need to find the tiara before that Michelsandgelo van tears out of here at like five-thirty."

"Fine," said Pinky.

"We can circle back for the towels later," said Mr. Ortega, placing his hand on Pinky's shoulder. "Right now, we need to play with a sense of urgency."

"So let's hit the beach," I said.

"Booyah!" said Gloria.

The five of us strode across the patio and onto the beach path—where we had to stop.

Because Pinky Nelligan was mobbed by several dozen adoring fans.

Have I mentioned how super famous he's become? It's great, but it can really slow you down, especially when you're in a hurry.

And . . . Action!

Finally (okay, twenty minutes later), our little movie crew made it down to the Surf Monkey sand sculpture.

"Hey, you're that kid!" said Travis when he saw Pinky. "From the movie!"

"Can I take a selfie with you?" asked Darryl, pulling out his phone—the same phone he swore Jimbo had stolen when, now that I thought about it, he probably just hid it in that basket thingy and had Travis call his number while the deputies were talking to Jimbo.

Plus, Travis was the one who had made me suspicious of Jimbo in the first place!

I tried not to let any of those thoughts show on my face. I had to be like Pinky. I had to be an actor!

Pinky posed for the selfie.

"What's with the camera crew?" asked Travis.

"We're producing a documentary!" announced Grandpa. "I'm the producer. That means I'm putting up the cash, but, hey, I don't mind, because this, my friends, is a project I truly believe in."

Fact: I've learned a ton about showmanship and spinning a story from my grandfather, the one and only Walt Wilkie. For instance, to really sell a tale, you need specifics and telling details. That's what makes fiction seem so real.

"We're very fortunate to have the legendary Manuel Ortega as our director of photography," Grandpa continued. "I'm sure you've seen his work on TV."

Mr. Ortega lowered the camera and smiled. "Weeknights at eleven."

"My grandson, P. T. Wilkie," said Grandpa, "is our director."

"Really?" said Travis. "He's just a kid."

"It might run on one of those family channels they have on cable first," said Grandpa. "And who knows what a family likes to watch better than a kid with a family? P.T.? Take it away."

Yep. Grandpa was handing the story off to me.

"This movie," I explained, "is all about the artists who travel the coastline of this great nation, sculpting art out of sand. The geniuses we call"—I framed the air with my hands—"the sand hoppers!"

"Aren't those fleas?" said Travis.

"No. They're itinerant craftsmen, moving from beach to beach, practicing their craft and sculpting their masterpieces."

Travis and Darryl looked at each other proudly.

"Well," said Darryl, "we are kind of special."

"We need someone to follow," I said, looking around the beach at some of the other sculptures and the artists who created them. "Who to pick? So many artists to choose from."

"Do us!" said Darryl. "I always wanted to be on TV."

"I guess we are kind of special," said Travis.

"And that's why America wants to get to know you better," said Pinky, stepping forward, holding a microphone.

"Let's roll video," I said.

"Roll video!" echoed Gloria, acting as my assistant director.

"Video is rolling!" announced Mr. Ortega.

(We all learned a lot of movie lingo hanging out with the crew that shot *Beach Party Surf Monkey*.)

"Tell us about this sculpture," said Pinky with a wink. "He sure looks familiar."

"Because it's your costar," said Travis, "Surf Monkey himself. It is our crowning achievement. Best we've ever done at any sand sculpture competition."

Darryl giggled. "You can say that again."

After about fifteen more minutes of questions and answers, I called, "Cut!"

"Cut!" cried Gloria.

"That's a cut," said her dad.

"Bee-yoo-tee-full!" said Grandpa.

"When's this going to be on TV?" asked Travis with a slightly worried look on his face.

"Not anytime soon," I told him. "We have to shoot a lot of B-roll of the sculptures. Edit. Mix in the music, add some sound effects, tweak the color—"

Travis grinned. "Good. Take your time."

"Those were some good questions, Pinky," said Darryl.

"Thanks, man."

"And you guys gave great answers," I said. "But . . ."

"But what?" said Gloria.

"What's wrong, man?" asked Pinky.

"Is there a problem?" said Grandpa.

"Come on, kid," said Travis. "Out with it."

"Something's missing. It needs a little extra oomph. Like on *Shark Tank* when they give you the up-close-and-personal backstory. When they go to the entrepreneur's home so you can take a behind-the-scenes peek at his or her everyday life and dreams . . ."

Darryl nodded. "It's awesome when they do that."

I kept going. "I wish we had a real behind-the-scenes feel for what it's like to be a sand hopper. If only we could show America how and where these artistic geniuses live when they're on the road . . . What kind of food is in their refrigerators? How many socks do they need to pack because they're always getting sand in their shoes?"

I took a deep breath.

I'd baited my line.

I just hoped the fish were biting.

64

The Key to Finding the Tiara

"**Y**ou guys can film up in our room," said Travis. "Just watch out for the dirty socks under the bed."

Travis tossed me the key to room 230—giving me all the permission I needed to go in and search for the missing tiara.

This thing was going to work.

"You want us to come up with you?" asked Darryl. "Point out a few things of interest? I have this one souvenir T-shirt from Myrtle Beach. . . ."

"We don't mind showing you around up there," said Travis. "Both of us don't need to stay down here with the sculpture."

Oh-kay. I hadn't thought about this little wrinkle. Everybody was staring at me. Grandpa, Gloria, Mr. Ortega, Pinky. Even a couple of kids licking drippy ice-cream cones.

"Oh, yes you do need to stay," I said. "Mr. Conch gave me a quick heads-up."

"About what?" asked Travis.

"The best-in-show voting. They can't close voting at five, tally everything up, and give out the trophies at five-thirty."

"So?"

"So they've already counted up all the votes cast so far. You guys are like ten votes away from scoring the top trophy. Talk about a big, boffo ending for our documentary." I framed the air again. "You two. Silhouetted against the setting sun. Holding yet another trophy in your hands . . ."

"But that will only happen if you interface with your audience," said Gloria. "In today's highly competitive marketplace, you need to maximize customer contact and satisfaction."

Travis nodded. "We need to do some old-fashioned social networking. Face-to-face-style."

"Exactly," said Gloria. "Win, baby, win."

"Oh, we're planning on it," said Darryl.

The two sand sculptors knocked knuckles and went back to glad-handing and schmoozing every spectator who wandered by.

I headed up to room 230 with my movie crew.

We were after our own trophy: a diamond-studded tiara!

A Room with a View

"**Y**ou kids go inside," said Grandpa when we were on the balcony outside 230. "Mr. Ortega and I will stand guard out here."

"You have to believe in yourselves when you go in there, kids," said Mr. Ortega. "You three can flat-out play!"

"Riiight," said Gloria. "Thanks for that, Dad. Open the door, P.T."

Just to be super official, I used the room key Travis had given me.

Pinky, Gloria, and I went to work.

We opened all the drawers in the dresser.

We looked under both beds.

And sort of wished we hadn't.

"Do all guys kick their dirty underpants under the bed?"

Looks like they ordered their pizza with mushrooms.

"Well, they *are* called *under*pants," I said.

"Ewwww," said Gloria. "Hurry up. Look somewhere else."

Pinky was checking out the closet.

"Nothing in here, either, you guys," he said.

We searched for another ten minutes. We swapped places. Pinky checked under the beds. Gloria and I did the closet, the dressers, and the bathroom.

Nothing.

Except somebody needed to remind Darryl and Travis to occasionally flush their toilet. Seriously. Nobody wants to see that.

"No wonder they didn't mind us snooping around," said Gloria after we made our fourth and final sweep through the room. "The tiara isn't up here."

"Are you sure they stole it?" asked Pinky.

"I used to be," said Gloria.

"I still am." I went to the curtains and pulled back an edge.

I could see Travis and Darryl working the crowd at their sand sculpture, probably telling everybody it was their "crowning achievement," since that seemed to be their favorite way to describe their creation.

Crowning achievement!

Of course! That was why they'd slept down on the beach instead of in their room on Sunday night.

They were protecting their buried treasure.

"They definitely stole the tiara," I told my friends. "We're just looking for it in the wrong place."

Poseidon's Crown

"They hid it in plain sight," I announced.

"Huh?" said Pinky.

"They buried the stolen tiara inside Poseidon's crown! That's why they were camping out down by the sculpture last night."

"They were?" said Gloria.

"Yeah. I paid them a visit pretty close to midnight. They had a little fire, sleeping bags. . . ."

"Aren't beach fires, like, illegal?" said Pinky.

"So is tiara snatching," I replied.

I tapped on the glass and motioned for Grandpa and Mr. Ortega to join us inside the room.

"What's up?" said Grandpa. "Did you find the tiara?"

"Yes and no," I said.

"So we're calling an audible?" said Mr. Ortega. "Going with a change-up?"

I had no idea what Mr. Ortega was talking about.

"What's our new plan, P.T.?" asked Gloria.

"Okay. I think Travis stole the tiara from the butler's room, buried it in his sand bucket, carried it down to the beach, and hid it right where everybody could see it: on top of Poseidon's head!"

"Maybe this is why they've never been caught before!" said Gloria. "They always hid their loot inside their sand sculptures, where nobody thought to look."

"Exactly!" I said.

"They've done this sort of thing before?" asked Mr. Ortega.

"We think so," said Gloria. "For years, there's been a string of unsolved burglaries at beach resorts where Travis and Darryl just happened to be competing in sand sculpture festivals."

"We need to lure Travis and Darryl away from the Surf Monkey sculpture," I said.

"Unfortunately," said Gloria, "we just convinced them they had to stay with their masterpiece to glad-hand voters."

"Right. So we're going to need something extremely powerful to tempt them away."

"What?" said Grandpa. "Some more BeDazzled headgear?"

"No," I said. "The best burgers on the beach."

"Um, nothing personal, kiddo, but you don't make those so good."

"I know. That's why I need to call Jimbo."

Well-Done Burgers

"**H**ey, man. What's up? How are things in Wonderland?"

Surprisingly, Jimbo sounded like his usual laid-back self when I called him at his apartment, which was just a mile or so away from the motel.

"Terrible."

"Still losin' business because someone who wasn't me stole that tiara, huh?"

"And because my cooking stinks."

"No worries. We can fix that, man. You just need a few lessons."

"No," I said. "What I really need is a new brain."

"Huh?"

"How could I ever think you'd steal something out of a guest's room?"

"Well, you had that video. I probably would've

thought the same thing if I'd seen a clip of you banging on a door and digging in your pocket for a passkey. Or I might've thought, 'Whoa, that dude really needs to use the bathroom, bad.'"

"No. You would've given me the benefit of the doubt. Because everybody who works at the Wonderland is family. And that's what families do: they stick up for each other."

There was a long pause.

I think I heard Mr. Ortega sniffle behind me. He's a pretty emotional guy, especially for a super-macho sports reporter.

"Dude?" said Jimbo. "Are you, like, trying to apologize?"

"Yeah. I've been doing a lot of that lately."

"Well, P.T.," said Jimbo, "we all make mistakes. That's why most pencils have erasers on 'em."

"Can you come back to the Banana Shack and whip up a couple of your Surf Monkey burgers? Can you do it, like, right now?"

"Man, you must really be hungry."

"They're not for me. They're for the two guys we think really stole the tiara."

"For real? And you want me to make these two dudes a hot lunch? Wow. When you had me arrested, I didn't even get a cold order of fries to go."

"I know, but—"

"Aw, I'm just messin' with you, man. I'll be right over. Just need to remember where I put my shoes. . . ."

"Great. Oh, can you stop by the grocery store on the way? We're out of beef. And hamburger buns. We need pickles, too. . . ."

Jimbo laughed and said he'd be firing up the grill in "two shakes of a bunny's tail." I figured it would really take him like thirty minutes.

Which was perfect.

"Now I need to call Jack Alberto," I said.

"Who's he?" asked Grandpa.

"Friend of ours from school," said Pinky.

"He has a metal detector," said Gloria.

"One of those wands you wave over the sand to find buried treasure?" asked Mr. Ortega.

I grinned. "Exactly. I figure our missing tiara has to have some kind of metal in it to hold all those diamonds and pearls in place."

The Family Plan

I speed-dialed Jack.

"You need me anymore?" asked Pinky. "I'm supposed to do this interview thing for my new movie. . . ."

"We're good," I said. "Thanks for everything."

We fist-bumped. So did he and Gloria.

"So long, Pinky," said Grandpa.

"Hasta la vista, baby," said Mr. Ortega.

"Hey," said Pinky, "I should use that line in my next flick!"

He left. Jack answered his phone.

"Hey, Jack? P. T. Wilkie," I said.

"Hey, P.T. What's up?"

"We need you to bring your metal detector to our beach."

"Cool. Did you guys bury some coins, like I suggested?"

"Nope. Something better."

"Do I get to keep it when I find it?"

"Um, not exactly. But we'll give you a trophy. And a free burger."

There was a pause.

"And one for Nate," said Jack.

"Your little brother?"

"Yo, if I don't get to keep the buried treasure . . ."

"Fine. Two burgers. With fries. Plus a Sproke."

"*Cherry* Sprokes. For both of us."

"Fine."

"Deal!"

● ● ●

Jimbo made it to the motel first. He was hugging two huge sacks of groceries, which he set down on a table when Mom came out of the laundry room carrying another basket of clean linen.

"Jimmy," said Mom. "It's great to see you again."

"Ditto," said Jimbo, shooting Mom a wink.

"We're all so sorry about—"

Jimbo held up his hand. "I know. P.T. told me. Repeatedly. But if you folks need help, I'm your man. We're family, Wanda."

"What's in the bags?"

"Burger stuff."

"Did we run out of meat?"

"Yep. Just like at the Happy Ox. Remember?"

"How could I forget? I was a waitress, you were the lead line cook . . ."

"And I sent you over to that burger joint next door to pick up a crate of their frozen quarter-pound patties. I cooked 'em up, made 'em look fancy with parsley sprigs, and swore it was chopped sirloin! Good times."

"Yeah," said Mom.

Then she laughed, something I hadn't seen her do all weekend long.

Metal Detectives

"Well," said Jimbo, "I'd better fire up the grill."

"Thanks for coming back, Jimmy."

"You're welcome, Wanda."

Jimbo hauled his groceries behind the Banana Shack bar and went to work.

"So," I said to Mom, "is that why you hired Jimbo to be our chef? You knew him when you were waitressing?"

"Yeah," she said with a far-off look in her eye. "Back in the day."

"Cool. And, Mom?"

"Yeah, hon?"

"Everything's going to be okay. I promise."

"Great. Then maybe Clara will come back and help me make all those beds upstairs."

Mom hauled the heavy laundry basket up to the second floor.

Jimbo slapped the first burger patties on the grill.

"Mmm," said Grandpa, coming out of his workshop with Mr. Ortega and the pair of oscillating fans I'd asked them to dig up. "Those burgers smell delicious."

"Indeed they do," added Mr. Ortega.

"Jimbo, can you make me one with a slice of bologna on top instead of bacon strips?" Grandpa asked. "We could call it a bologna cheeseburger!"

"Fer sure, Walt. No problemo. It would pair nicely with a cold can of Cel-Ray."

"Don't I know it!"

"Hey, you guys!"

Jack and his younger brother Nate came around the corner, toting their metal-detecting gear.

"Sorry we're late," said Jack. "Dad had trouble fitting the X15 into his trunk."

"I told him it had to go in sideways," said Nate. "Duh."

Do you think you could find my missing can of Cel-Ray with that thing?

"So, P.T., the entire team is on the field," said Mr. Ortega. "Burgers are sizzling on the grill. Who throws the first ball?"

"You and Gloria," I said. "I need you guys to rig up those fans."

"On it," said Gloria and her dad.

"Point them toward the Gulf," I instructed. "I want to bombard the beach with the irresistible aroma of juicy charbroiled beef!"

"It'll make everybody drool," said Grandpa, sniffing the meaty perfume already wafting on the breeze. "My mouth is watering so much I think my tongue is turning into a Slip 'N Slide!"

"Well, you and Mr. Ortega get first dibs on the burgers," I said.

"Oooh," said Grandpa. "I like this plan. Do we get to eat our burgers first, too?"

"Of course. But not until after you're down on the beach, offering to take over the crowd-schmoozing duties for Darryl and Travis while they come up to grab their free burgers from Jimbo."

"Got it," said Grandpa. "They see our burgers, they smell the ones sizzling on the grill—*boom!* They abandon their posts. What're you kids going to do on the beach while the two schnooks are up here?"

I grinned. "We're going treasure hunting with Jack and Nate!"

Burgers on the Breeze

As predicted, a minute after Grandpa and Mr. Ortega traipsed down to the beach, Travis and Darryl came hiking up to the Banana Shack, their noses wiggling as they sniffed the burger-scented air.

"Hey, dudes!" called Jimbo, casually aiming one of the fans so it would send some more grill smoke straight over to Travis and Darryl. "Can I interest you two in a free Surf Monkey burger?"

"You bet," said Travis. "We smelled 'em all the way down on the beach."

"Is that a fact?" said Jimbo. "Well, like my grandmother used to say, paint me green and call me a pickle."

Jimbo cranked up the volume on his steel drum music, just like I'd asked him to. It would drown out any noise we might make down on the beach when we started scanning the Poseidon sand sculpture with Jack's metal detector.

And when we ripped the crown off the Greek sea god's head.

"You guys on a break?" Jimbo asked.

"Yeah," said Darryl as he and Travis sat on adjoining barstools. "The old man and the TV guy are down on the beach, dealing with our fans."

"Here you go, boys," said Jimbo, sliding plates onto the counter. "You want fries?"

Travis and Darryl nodded. They couldn't say yes, because both their mouths were full of mashed meat. I could tell that Jimbo had made their burgers extra large so they'd be extra sloppy and take longer to scarf down.

While they ate, Jack, Nate, Gloria, and I tiptoed away from the Banana Shack with the X15.

We had some metal to detect.

Caution: Nerds at Work

We hurried down to the Surf Monkey display.

Grandpa and Mr. Ortega were, of course, already there—talking to Mr. Conch. A crowd of spectators strolled past, admiring Travis and Darryl's craftsmanship.

"What's Mr. Conch doing there?" asked Gloria.

"I don't know," I told her. "Probably telling people not to vote for us. Come on. It's showtime!"

I took up a position right in front of the massive Poseidon statue. Jack's metal detector thrummed in my hands.

"Ladies and gentlemen, boys and girls," I announced, "for years, my friends and I have combed these beaches with our metal detectors, searching for buried treasure."

"Because you're nerds!" boomed Mr. Conch. "It's true. Sad, but true."

"You're right, Mr. Conch," I said. "Sad. Because for years, my friends and I have found nothing on this beach with our metal detectors besides a few toy cars, a couple nickels, and an empty tuna can. But today, ladies and gentlemen, is our lucky day. Treasure has returned to St. Pete Beach!"

"Where is it?" shouted a kid.

"In this imported sand!" I pointed to the sand sculpture behind me.

Mr. Conch laughed. "What are you talking about, Petey? You sound as goofy as your crackpot grandfather!"

"I'm right here, Ed," said Grandpa. "I can hear you, you know."

"So? What's with all the treasure talk?"

"It's very simple, Mr. Conch," I said. "Thanks to you and the St. Pete Beach Lodging Association, this sand behind me came from beaches unknown. Beaches that have not yet been combed. Beaches where pirates probably buried treasure chests full of gold doubloons, diamonds, pearls, and other crown jewels! Just watch!"

I quickly swung the metal detector up to Poseidon's crown, keeping my eyes locked on the meter in the handgrip.

The needle didn't swing.

The detector didn't beep.

There wasn't anything metal on top of the sea god's head.

I couldn't believe it.

I was wrong again.

Or was I?

Because when I lowered the metal detector to the ground, down to the base of the statue, it started pinging like crazy!

Sand Grabs

"What do you think you're doing, kid?"

Travis was back. Darryl, too.

The two of them were charging down the sloping beach.

Jimbo was right behind them.

He leapt forward and tackled Darryl.

"Get away from my masterpiece!" shouted Travis, wiping his greasy hands on his shorts.

Meanwhile, Jimbo sat on the squirming Darryl and kept him pinned to the sand. The more Darryl swung his arms and legs, the deeper he snow-angeled himself into the beach.

Jimbo had taken one angry artiste out of the equation. We just had to deal with Travis.

As soon as all the shouting had started, Mr. Conch had slipped away.

I raised the metal detector as if it were a base-ball bat, and lined up a shot to bust up Surf Monkey's board.

"Whoa!" said Jack, grabbing the thing out of my hands. "That's a very sensitive electronic instrument. You can't bang stuff with it."

Smirking, Travis strutted closer.

"Step away from the sand sculpture, son. You knock it down, you won't win best in show. That might be what your motel needs to make people forget your bad cooking and your maid's sticky fingers. So I'll only say this one more time: step away from my masterpiece."

I laughed.

"This sand sculpture doesn't belong to you, Mr. Shelton."

Travis gave me a "How did you know my last name?" look.

"We paid you to build it for us. So guess what? We can turn it into a giant sand piñata if we want to! Because avast and ahoy, me hearties, there's buried treasure inside it!"

I dropped to my knees and started digging.

"Awesome!" said Jack. "You took my idea and made it even better! You hid treasures *inside* the sand sculpture! This is so cool!"

He swung the metal detector across Surf Monkey's feet.

"There's something down there! Something big!"

Now all the spectators in the crowd fell to their knees and started tearing apart the sand sculpture.

Travis couldn't take it.

"You little brats! Leave my sand alone!"

Grandpa and Mr. Ortega blocked his lunge forward.

"Uh-uh-uh," said Grandpa. "We paid ten thousand dollars for that sand sculpture, Mr. Michelsandgelo. The kids can tear it up if they want to."

"B-b-but . . ."

"FYI," added Mr. Ortega, puffing up his chest, "before I was a sportscaster, I was a professional athlete. I can still bench-press . . . you!"

Demolition Derby

"Stop them!" shouted Travis. "Those brats are destroying a priceless work of art. Do something!"

"You know, Travis," said Grandpa, "maybe you're right. Maybe we should do something. Manny? How about you call the cops? Their number is 911."

"Good idea," said Mr. Ortega, pulling out his phone.

"Oh, wait," said Grandpa. "I forgot. The deputies are already here. Because the lodging association asked the Pinellas County Sheriff's Office to help us handle crowd control."

Two sheriff's deputies strolled up the beach.

"What's going on, Walt?" asked one.

"You know me, Brian," said Grandpa. "Just having a little wacky fun in the sun. Why build a sand castle if you can't knock it down?"

Travis didn't even try to contradict Grandpa. He did, however, try to take a step backward and disappear.

That was when Mr. Ortega grabbed hold of him by the arm.

I clawed at the sand like a dog in a hurry to hide its bone.

Jack swept my sand hole with his detector. I heard pings beeping closer and closer together.

"Three more inches!" Jack shouted.

I kept scooping out sand.

My fingertips snagged the hard edge of something bumpy.

It wasn't a seashell or a can of Dr. Brown's Cel-Ray soda.

It was the Twittleham Tiara!

My Crowning Achievement

The sheriff's deputies detained Travis and Darryl while we waited for Lord Pettybone to join us at the sand heap formerly known as Surf Monkey and Poseidon.

Gloria and her dad raced up to their rooms to retrieve his video camera. I texted Mom to let her know what was going on.

She texted back that she had to make a quick call first and then she'd be right down.

I wanted Mr. Ortega to record some new video clips when His Lordship arrived. Grandpa volunteered to head over to the Conch Reef Resort and summon the royal family out of their royal suite.

Meanwhile, Jimbo went back to the Banana Shack to make everybody celebratory cheeseburgers.

Grandpa escorted the Pettybone family across

the beach to what was left of our sand sculpture exhibit. Digby, the butler, was behind them, holding up a mammoth umbrella for shade.

People in the crowd snapped photographs.

The royal family gave them all one of those royal lightbulb-changer backward waves.

Mr. Ortega stood by with the camcorder propped on his shoulder.

"Oh, my," gasped Lady Lilly. "Whatever happened to Surf Monkey and Poseidon?"

"They had to go," I said, pointing to the tiara sitting in the hole where Surf Monkey's waves used to be. "They were covering up the truth."

"That's it!" cried Lady Lilly. "My tiara!"

"Huzzah!" exclaimed His Lordship.

"Brilliant!" added his wife.

"Well played," said Digby. "Well played, indeed."

"That's a positive ID," declared one of the sheriff's deputies. "Give us your wrists, gentlemen."

Travis and Darryl, who were kneeling in the sand, tucked their hands behind their butts so the sheriff's deputies could handcuff them.

"Well done, Deputies," said Lord Pettybone. "Well done, indeed!"

"It wasn't us," said one of the deputies. "Young P. T. Wilkie here cracked the case."

"Is that true?" asked Lady Pettybone.

"It wasn't just me," I told her. "A whole lot of

people worked together to clear Clara's good name. Why, you might ask? Because family looks out for family!"

Mom joined us. Clara was with her.

"You remember Mrs. Rodriguez," Gloria said to Lord Pettybone. She leaned in. "Don't you?"

He dropped his chin a little. "N'yes. Indeed I do."

"You said some pretty mean stuff about her," I reminded him.

"N'yes. Frightfully sorry about all that."

"You said it on TV."

"N'yes. I suppose I did."

I nodded toward Mr. Ortega and his camera.

"Want to take it all back? On TV?"

"Indubitably."

"Huh?"

"That means yes, P.T.," Gloria whispered.

"Oh. Cool. Mr. Ortega? Roll video!"

Then Mr. Ortega pulled the trigger. "Hey, hey, Tampa Bay. Let's get to it!"

"Aaaaand . . . action!" I pointed at Lord Snooty-pants.

"Um, hello, this is Lord Pettybone, Marquess of Herferrshire."

"That's higher than an earl but lower than a duke, correct?" said Mr. Ortega behind the camera.

"Quite so." His Lordship went on to tell the camera, "I am terribly ashamed of my previous comments regarding Mrs. Clara Rodriguez, whom

I falsely accused of stealing our priceless family heirloom."

In fact, he found about five very different, very British ways to say he was sorry.

Finally, he turned to Clara and said, "I hope that one day, Mrs. Rodriguez, you will find it in your heart to forgive me."

"I will," said Clara, smiling next to Mom. "One day. Probably tomorrow."

Mom had called Clara the instant I let her know we'd found the tiara and discovered that our sand sculptors were the real thieves.

"Thank you, P.T.!" Clara said. She hugged me.

"You're welcome," I told her, even though it was kind of hard to speak; she was hugging me so hard.

"Now," said Clara when she released me from her vise grip, "let's have a fiesta!"

"Woo-hoo!" I shouted.

Clara hugged Gloria. And Grandpa. And Gloria's dad. What can I say? The lady's a hugger.

"Can we stay for burgers, too?" asked Jack.

"You bet," I said. "Plus, I still owe you guys some fries and a pair of Cherry Sprokes."

We all headed up the beach toward the motel.

That was when Travis shouted, "Wait!"

And Now a Word from Their Sponsor

"If I'm going to jail," said Travis, his hands cuffed behind his back, "I'm not going alone."

"I know," said Darryl. "I'm going with you."

"I'm not talking about you," said Travis. "I'm talking about him!" He bobbed his head sort of southward, toward the towering Conch Reef Resort building. "Conch!"

Okay. He definitely had my attention. The sheriff's deputies', too.

"What do you mean?" asked one.

Mr. Ortega switched on his camcorder.

"Mind if I record this?" he asked.

"Not at all," said Travis. "How's my hair?"

Mr. Ortega shot him a thumbs-up. "Hey, hey, Tampa Bay. Let's get to it!"

Travis cleared his throat.

"I have a confession to make," he said to the lens. "Edward Conch, the real estate tycoon, hired us to ruin his neighbors' business. He said he'd pay us fifty thousand dollars to stir up trouble at Walt Wilkie's Wonderland Motel."

"Said he'd give us free spa credits, too," added Darryl. "He has a sweet resort down near Fort Myers. Me and Travis did a gig there once."

"Where you stole stuff from hotel rooms!" I said, remembering that story we had found.

"Not from Conch's resort," said Travis. "Well, we did. But we put it all back."

"Because he caught us," said Darryl. "Twelve years ago, the man was definitely on the cutting edge of security-camera technology. Recorded everything from every angle."

"He's the one who told us to leave Florida and never come back," said Travis. "So imagine my surprise when he called me up. Offered us this gig. Said all we had to do was make it look like your motel was seedy. That your maids had sticky fingers."

He turned to Clara, who was glaring at him.

"Sorry about that, ma'am."

Travis was trying to be charming again.

It wasn't working.

"Usted es un hombre horrible," said Clara.

I couldn't wait to ask my Spanish teacher what *that* meant, because it sure didn't sound pretty.

"And then," Travis continued, "we hit the jackpot. The royal jewels rolled into the very motel we were hired to burglarize. Conch said we could keep whatever we stole—even your tiara."

"It was so easy to boost, too," added Darryl. "Travis was on his binoculars and saw Lady Lilly prancing around in the butler's room, wearing the tiara. So he went upstairs to pick the lock while I set up a fireworks display to attract her attention."

"If the fireworks didn't work," said Travis, "we probably would've blasted the soundtrack to *Beach Party Surf Monkey*."

"Oh, I love that music!" gushed Lady Lilly.

"We know," said Travis. "You told every newspaper and TV reporter in Florida how 'thrilled' you were to be staying in the 'very same' motel where they filmed your favorite movie. Quick tip? Next time you leave jewelry sitting on a couch, close the curtains *and* the door."

Lady Lilly sniffed a little. "Point taken."

"Once we had the tiara," Travis continued, "Conch was so happy, he gave us a bonus. He also told us to butter up you two junior detectives." He nodded at Gloria and me. "Said we should pretend to be your friends. Throw you off the scent."

"Until we didn't need to no more," added Darryl.

Yep. Travis played me. Then again, he was the one in handcuffs, so I guess I played him, too.

One of the deputies took off his hat to scratch his head.

"Wait a second," he said. "If what you're saying about Mr. Conch is true . . ."

"Oh, it is true, and I can prove it," said Travis. "See, I learned a thing or two from Conch all those years ago in Fort Myers. Now, for security purposes, I record everything, too. Every phone call, every text message, every email. I have enough evidence to send our co-conspirator away for ten, maybe fifteen years."

The sheriff's deputy pulled the radio microphone off his shoulder board.

"Carolyn? This is Josh. We're gonna need another squad car and an extra set of handcuffs. We need to arrest Edward Conch."

Family Fiesta

Jimbo pumped some party music out of the Banana Shack speakers and tossed a bag of coconut-crusted popcorn shrimp into the deep fryer.

"Everything's on the house!" Grandpa announced.

Mom and Clara sat at the bar, sipping Sprokes.

"This is delicious," said Clara.

"Mine's a Dr. Sproker!" joked Mom.

She and Clara laughed—the kind of big, hearty laugh I hadn't heard from either of them since, well, the previous week. Before Mr. Conch hatched his sleazy scheme to shut down the Wonderland. Before Travis and Darryl stole the Twittleham Tiara out of our Cassie McGinty Suite.

Well, guess what? It didn't work.

We heard the patrol cars come to take Mr. Conch away.

"He'll probably lawyer up," I said, because, as you know, I watch way too many cop shows on TV.

"He'll also probably go out of business," said Gloria. "Dad cut together Travis's confession footage and raced it down to WTSP, where they're already interrupting the regular programming to run it under a 'breaking news' banner. Conch stock will plummet."

Lord Pettybone felt so bad for what he had (almost) done to Clara's reputation that he quickly worked out a deal with Disney World and announced that the Twittleham Tiara would be "on exclusive display at the Wonderland Motel for two weeks before heading to the Magic Kingdom."

That's right. Disney would have to wait.

I don't think I'd ever seen Grandpa look so happy.

"We'll display it with *our* mouse!" he announced. "We can put it on top of Morty. That'll show 'em!"

"What about security?" I asked.

"Mr. Digby can chain Morty to his wrist!"

While the party rocked on, I slipped behind the counter to help Jimbo serve the second course: fresh peel-and-eat shrimp and oysters, the kind that wouldn't make people puke.

"Thanks again for everything," I told him.

"You're welcome, little man. Hey, I had, like, an idea. If Mr. Conch really does go out of business, maybe you guys could buy his property next door and put in that fourteen-story-tall waterslide you were talking about the other day."

"Nah. That's okay. We don't need the Conch Reef Resort. The Wonderland is pretty great the way it is. So, did you and Mom really fool people into thinking quarter pounders from a burger joint were chopped sirloin?"

"What can I say, P.T.? Guess I'm a little like you. I can spin a good story when I need to."

I perked up.

"When exactly was this?"

"I don't know. Maybe like twelve, thirteen years ago."

"Where were you guys working? Here in St. Pete?"

"Nah. We were both over in Orlando. Steak joint outside Disney World called the Happy Ox. It was your mom's second job. She's always been a hard worker."

He looked at Grandpa, who was chatting with

our Canadian guest, Ms. Nelson. "Her day job was at Disney World." He put a finger to his lips.

"It's okay," I said. "Grandpa already knows."

"And he forgave her?"

"Yeah. I think she said she was sorry about a billion times."

Jimbo grinned. "Guess it runs in the family, huh?"

I ate some popcorn shrimp, gobbled down a bowl of Freddy the Frog's Green Pond Scum ice cream, and tried to learn all the words to "Cheeseburger in Paradise" so Gloria and I could karaoke to it.

When I finally went to bed, I stared out the window at the stars, making up another story in my head, all about a young cook and a waitress, goofing around at a place in Orlando called the Happy Ox. Having each other's backs. Sharing secrets. Becoming family, even though they had different last names. It sounded like a lot of fun.

Almost as much fun as living in a motel.

Anyway, Dad, if you're reading this, I hope you realize what you've been missing all these years.

We're having a wonderful time at the Wonderland.

Wish you were here.

Or who knows—maybe you already are.

P. T. Wilkie's
Outrageously
Ridiculous
and
Occasionally
Useful
Stuff

P.T. and Gloria's
Fact or Fiction Quiz:
Beach Blanket Edition!

(Circle your answer and find out if you're correct at ChrisGrabenstein.com.)

1. The world's tallest sand castle was built in Florida, the very same state where the Wonderland is!
FACT or FICTION

2. The art of building sand castles has been around for hundreds of years.
FACT or FICTION

3. Coney Island is known for the Nathan's Famous International Hot Dog Eating Contest. At the 2017 contest, Joey Chestnut set a new record by eating fifty-five hot dogs!
FACT or FICTION

4. Sand sculpting gained popularity after a man created a sand sculpture of a woman and a baby in 1897 in Atlantic City, New Jersey.
FACT or FICTION

5. In the 1700s, ladies' swimsuits included jackets!
FACT or FICTION

6. Myrtle Beach, in South Carolina, is full of restaurants that host eating challenges: if you finish the food, it's free!

FACT or FICTION

7. Beach sand can be a rainbow of different colors—white, gray, red, purple, pink, and even black!

FACT or FICTION

8. Legend says that the Nathan's Famous competition began on July 4, 1916, when four immigrants held a hot dog eating contest to settle an argument about who was the most patriotic.

FACT or FICTION

9. Even though seagulls are always found around beaches, they can't drink ocean water.

FACT or FICTION

10. The very first version of sunscreen was created in the 1930s.

FACT or FICTION

Sandapalooza
Sand-Sculpting Tips That'll Blow the Sand Right Out of Your Shorts!

1. Bring Sunblock: Protecting yourself from the sun's rays is more important than any sand castle or sculpture. So before you start to sculpt, dip yourself in sunscreen like a cookie in a glass of milk!

2. Be Prepared or Be Square: Never start working without a plan of what you want to build. And every sand architect needs some handy dandy tools to make the perfect castle! So, make sure you bring a pail, a sand scooper, and, if you're feeling artsy, a sand sculptor brush to help you really put in some fine details.

3. Go Big or Go Home: Always start with a pile of sand that's a bit larger than what you think you'll need. Since sand sculptures are created by removing all the sand that's not part of the creation, you've gotta make sure there's ample sand to use from the get-go.

4. Keep the Sand Wet and Your Shorts Dry: Wet sand is happy sand! If you want your sculpture to hold its shape, then the sand has to be wet. I'm not talking drizzle wet—I'm talking thunderstorm wet. Hurricane wet. Water-balloon-fight wet. Got it? Good.

5. **Pack the Sand Like It's a Suitcase and You Only Get to Take One:** The tighter you pack the sand, the better your structure will hold together. Pat it down, pound it, beat it, smack it.

6. **Let's Take It from the Top!** Always build from the top down. You don't want to ruin the details below or have to reclean completed sections.

7. **Teamwork Makes the Dream Work:** Sand sculpting is fun on your own, but it's even more awesome with a friend or two! Get some buddies together and divide and conquer. A castle's a big place; why not share it?

Acknowledgments

A big THANK-YOU (and a gallon jug of orange juice) to the behind-the-scenes crew that keeps the Wonderland humming: Barbara Bakowski, eagle-eyed copyeditor; Linda Camacho, authenticity consultant and adviser; Shana Corey, wonderful editor; Nicole de las Heras, director de la art; Maya Motayne, editorial assistant; Michelle Nagler, on-premises associate publishing director; Eric Myers, agent extraordinaire; and J. J. Myers—first reader and first love.

CHRIS GRABENSTEIN is the #1 *New York Times* bestselling author of *Escape from Mr. Lemoncello's Library, Mr. Lemoncello's Library Olympics, Mr. Lemoncello's Great Library Race, The Island of Dr. Libris,* the Welcome to Wonderland series, and many other books, as well as the coauthor of numerous fun and funny page-turners with James Patterson, including the I Funny, House of Robots, and Treasure Hunters series, *Word of Mouse,* and *Jacky Ha-Ha.* Chris grew up going to St. Petersburg, Florida, every summer and loved visiting roadside attractions like Gatorland, the fabulous Tiki Gardens, Weeki Wachee Springs, and the "talking mermaids" at Webb's City. Chris lives in New York City with his wife, J.J. You can visit him at ChrisGrabenstein.com.

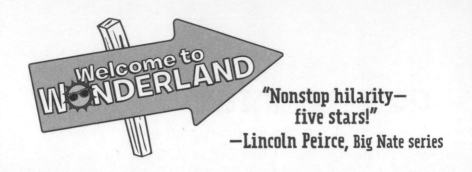

"Nonstop hilarity—
five stars!"
—Lincoln Peirce, Big Nate series

Read all the
Welcome to Wonderland
adventures!

And don't miss
Welcome to Wonderland 4,
coming in 2019!